BETWEEN

reality and insanity

a collection of eclectic speculative fiction tales

Melanie Rees

These are works of fiction.
All names, characters, places and events are a product of the author's imagination. Any similarities between places or persons, living or dead, is unintentional and coincidental.

First Printing, 2025
ISBN: 978-1-7640108-5-6

The author respectfully acknowledges the Traditional Owners of Australia as our first storytellers and creators of culture in the land from which many of these stories are inspired and acknowledges their continuing connection to Country. The author pays their respect to their culture and elders past, present and emerging.

Contents

Acknowledgements 4
Ephemeral love 5
No free returns 13
Colourblind 26
Feeding Time 32
Pass the parcel 43
The esky ghost 51
Shifting 63
From all that we flee 65
Hive mind 79
Silence Broken 91
Shadow harvest 98
The Red Goddess 107
Look inside 112
Elementability 115
Pre-emptive 130
Time to kill 133
Timely drop 136
The Dragon 140
Untitled 153
Tek-tonic 154
The Last Polar Bear 161
Bloodletting 177
Painting the sky 186
Attrition of the soul 187
Traditions 200
Story behind the stories 204

Acknowledgements

Ephemeral love: First published by The Future Fire in 2008
Silence broken: First published by Bards and Sages quarterly in 2012
Shadow harvest: First published by Third Flatiron's Terra, Tara, Terror in 2018
The red goddess: First published by Factor Four in 2018
Look inside: First published by So bad it's good anthology in 2018
Elementability: First published by Aurealis in 2016
Pre-emptive: First published by Antipodean SF in 2007
Time to kill: First published by Daily Science Fiction in 2011
Timely drop: First published by Neo-Opsis in 2017
The dragon: First published by Cosmos online in 2012
Untitled: First published by Apex in 2014
Tek-tonic: First published by Infinitas in 2008
The last polar bear: First published by Ecotrastrophe II in 2016
Bloodletting: First published by Unnerviing in 2019
Painting the sky: First published by Postcard stories in 2018
Attrition of the soul: First published by Crash code anthology in 2018
Traditions: First published by The Martian Wave in 2016

Ephemeral love

Deep within, something churns. A mechanical heartbeat pierces its way to the surface infringing upon the tranquillity, as the sun sinks and surrenders to the numinous night. Amphibians croak in the rich primordial swamps. A myriad of other creatures join in and impart their tunes to the exultant chorus.

In the distance, the silhouette of the mechanical down-shaft seems to be calling, almost beckoning. He stands on the precipice, loyalties divided between obligation and something else that remains undefined. He needs to remain here, to dwell in her golden aura, comforted by her tender melodies and vibrant hues. But his commitments seem to overshadow everything else. The masters of the underworld trigger something deep within; an instinctive mechanism tells him that he must abide.

In ungainly fashion, he lumbers towards the shaft. An opaque tubular carriage rises to the surface and with digits, of ill-designed dexterity, he programs the sequence that will take him to the lower levels of the ancient hibernaculum. The carriage doors close and stars vanish one by one, as he is plundered into darkness and vertical descent. The darkness is not soothing like the visual silence of the night sky, rather an unnatural emptiness: rigid and unmoving. Over the eons he has never felt the urge to unplug, to vanish. Perhaps this is what they once called fear. He flips an internal switch and tunes out to the black commotion.

#

The carriage opens and reawakens him. Trudging from the hateful elevator, ancient sensor lights are triggered, illuminating the vast antechamber. Although a thick film of dust has settled and a few rodents have taken up residency, it still looks like it did all those millions of years ago.

There are four walls, each sharing a certain grandeur, a certain regality: although they pale in comparison to "her'. The plasma-infused wall surrounding the down-shaft shines with thousands of images from an age long forgotten. He counted them once, only sixty two thousand, three hundred and seven relayed over and over again: images of people smiling out from the wall at him, people holding hands, children running under sprinklers and walking with bare feet on manicured grass. On the adjacent southern and northern walls lie two huge computer screens and consoles. They span the entire length of the antechamber, powered indirectly through the solar rays captured above. Data flickers across their black surface intermittently. At the other end of the antechamber, the hibernaculum entrance dwindles in the distance.

The tinny voice of the computer echoes within the empty auditorium monotonously, "DE-STASIS THAWING WILL COMMENCE IN TWO HOURS. PLEASE ACCEPT OR REJECT RE-COLONIZATION STATUS. DE-ATROPHYING PROCESS WILL COMMENCE IN SEVENTY-FOUR HOURS. PLEASE ACCEPT OR REJECT RE-COLONIZATION STATUS...DE-STASIS THAWING WILL COMMENCE IN TWO HOURS..." it continues its message repeatedly.

The whirring of the hibernaculum's de-thawing sequence starts up again, drowning out the computers tinkling and his own thoughts.

Sluggishly he wonders across to the computer terminal and mulls over the readings. Climatic trends scroll across the screen in iridescent green lettering.

"Atmospheric methane: 1600 parts per billion. Nitrous oxide: 280 parts per billion. Carbon dioxide: 290 parts per million. Re-colonisation status: 92.3% optimisation."

Why the re-colonisation percentage is below one hundred puzzles him. Perhaps they are waiting for trees bejewelled with gold leaves.

The whirring intensifies as the second stage recolonisation process kicks into gear. He can just make out the caskets of the hibernaculum, stacked in high, tiered columns, like a tomb. Above the entrance is a golden plaque engraved with the words "Buds for the Valley of New Eden." Soon these so-called buds will blossom across fields and hillsides. Their pollen will blow in the wind to the atmosphere and wash downstream to the oceans. Everywhere will be a mass of bipedal flowers and their pollen.

Masses of them once stood in this cryostat auditorium listening and waiting. They said he would need to remember the "love' humanity once shared and reaffirm belief in his duties.

Like all of history, he remembers it vividly, although he is still not sure that he understands.

#

The speaker sits next to him, adorned in full suit and tie, shielded from the scalding heat outside by the antechamber.

In an opulent voice, the suited man commands attention. "Do not fear my fellow citizens for our society will return. Yes, we will sleep, but we will re-awake. This fiery planet will cool, gases will dissipate, soils will become enriched, resources will become plentiful and...." The suited man's voice increases another 1.23 decibels as he raises his hands and looks up at the ceiling "And the rain... the *rain* my friends will fall like it once did."

Looking up at the featureless ceiling quizzically, he searches his databanks for information on rain and retrieves images of small children in oversized gumboots splashing in muddy puddles and gastropods leaving silvery trails in wet lawns.

"And watching over us will be the Guardian, the newest R65 designed to be capable of withstanding the Venusian-like climate, which our world is spiralling towards. He will ensure de-stasis occurs when our world is perfect again. He will endure and hence we will endure. And our economy and society will blossom like the fields of wild flowers that once graced our landscape."

The auditorium fills with rapture.

The suited man's voice mellows and he reels off instructions. "If everyone would like to make their way to the hibernaculum with your lottery ticket ready the stewards will usher you to your respective chambers."

Flanked by large men and a stately woman the suited man is ushered to his resting spot. A young woman half his age and with large belly hastens forward crying desperately.

Black suited men race forward "You don't even have a pass, miss please step back." They usher her away as she cries and clutches her stomach.

Slowly the crowds start filtering across the floor. Many are finely dressed with keepsakes and trinkets strung about their necks. Some are turned away from the chamber despite cries of consternation. People scramble impatiently creating a bottleneck at the entrance to the hibernaculum. A scuffle breaks out. Several brutish men in camouflaged trousers head towards the commotion. Shots ring out. The antagonist falls listlessly to the ground with a thud. Only a few young faces bother to turn around.

The commotion slowly dies down and the "future blooms', as the suited man calls them, close up in their stasis capsules like petals closing as the sun retreats from the sky.

#

The auditorium becomes cold. Lifeless. Centuries pass. The computer hums monotonously. There are no other sounds.

The carriage of the up-shaft takes him to the world above. He shambles sluggishly across the cracked clay pans to a nearby rock and awkwardly lowers himself into a sitting position. Topsoil blows into the air with gusty winds. The dusty haze picks up the rays of the scorching sun. The sky glows orange behind silhouetted buildings. He watches as the buildings crumple to the ground over hundreds of years.

#

Millennia pass. A sound chimes throughout his head, like something hitting metal. He looks up to the scorching sky and droplets of liquid splatter upon his outstretched hand. The water trickles at first and then the skies open unforgivingly. In between the clacked clay pans, a monocotyledon germinates. A tiny leaf blade emerges, twisting and turning, capturing the sun. Several more emerge. A fleshy homogenous green carpet spreads across the clay pan. Slowly other green gems sprout amongst the carpet. They become woody and grow tall. Far taller than him. Always reaching for the sun.

#

Millennia pass. The rock he sits on erodes with wind and rain. It turns to dust. He gets up and wanders across the valley. More rain falls and a pool forms downhill.

#

Millions of years pass. Tiny crustaceans jump and pirouette in the thin film of water. The pool grows and covers the entire valley floor. After an age undefined, it teems with life. Fish come to visit him at the lakes edge. He calls one of them Freddie. Small Diptera with delicate wings and slender legs tread lightly on the water. Freddie snaps at one with his elongated body and it sends ripples across the lake before he dives back down below. Freddie introduces him to his children, and his children's children's children. One of them has little growths on his flanks. The lake starts to become overcrowded. A great, great descendent of Freddie walks up the banks to meet him. Sedges and rushes grow, fringing the lake edge, sheltering her inhabitants as they sing to him at night. He sings back to her a reassuring lullaby. Who the lullaby is intended to reassure he is unsure. She seems to reassure him, with her light and dark, her music and tranquillity, her majestic curves and her tiny creatures.

He longs to see her again; he yearns for her tender breath and exposed soul.

#

"DE-STASIS THAWING WILL COMMENCE IN THIRTY MINUTES. PLEASE ACCEPT OR REJECT RE-COLONIZATION OPTIMISATION STATUS."

The mechanical intrusion whirrs into his thoughts, pierces his circuits. Addle-pated he looks again at the giant screen that towers forebodingly above him. He cannot argue with the figures, everything is indeed perfect. Long-term climatic conditions are stable, resources have renewed, and there are promising signs of life with fish, amphibians and birds flourishing again.

He dubiously mutters to himself. "After two million years humans have been in stasis everything is indeed perfect."

#

He emerges from the elevator. She is there to greet him. Her rich blue veins slink down into the hills. Two birds perform a pas des deux above the river as something scampers through the undergrowth. Her morning dew glistens with the clear sunlight as if a million shards of mirrored glass have been strewn across the valley. Unparalleled beauty. Perhaps this is what they once called love? No, this feeling is not a fleeting thing; it has grown over the ages. They could not possibly have a word to describe the way he feels for her.

The churning and whirring has ceased.

"So what do you think? Should I give them another million years?" he asks the sun-kissed hills and river.

She whispers back with an earthly sigh, shrouding him in a misty blanket.

"Okay, you are right, two million would be better," he replies and awkwardly makes his way to the horizon and beyond the valley of New Eden.

No free returns

10 December 2063

Dear Synthtech,

I purchased a Synth helper T-model from your company last year. I don't want to make a fuss, it has assisted me since my beloved Harold passed, but it has been acting odd the past few weeks.

It's hard to explain the specific fault. Sometimes I catch it staring as if studying me. When I look it turns away and continues its chores.

If you could send someone to service the Synth that would be most welcome.

Sincerely,

Mrs. Angela Pinkerton

#

19 December 2063

Dear Ms. Pinkerton,

Our T-model was specifically designed to observe its owner to detect anomalies in behaviour and potentially pre-empt medical emergencies. What you described sounds like typical behaviour. I don't believe it warrants a service at this stage.

We test all our Synth models against the latest industry standards, and we greatly appreciate your feedback. It will help us ensure our newest models are even more capable of helping you in the future.

Warmest regards,

Candice

Your local Synthtech representative

#

20 December 2063

Thanks Candice,

Like I said, I do not wish to make a fuss. I am reassured that it will notify the hospital if I should fall and am unable to get up myself. It just seems more intense than it used to be.

In the past week it even started mimicking some of my mannerisms. Only yesterday it held its hands as if holding an invisible teacup and saucer while we were watching television. My morning cuppa with Harold used to be my time to relax, but the Synth is giving me the creeps. I don't know how else to describe it. It seems "off' compared to its usually patient and cooperative self.

Sincerely,

Angela

#

11 January 2064

Dear Ms. Pinkerton,

We here at Synth-tech can assure you this is merely affectionate behaviour. As a valued customer, we can arrange for a crew to pick up the model. It is at least four months before its scheduled service, but we can run a diagnostic check for a nominal $500 early call out fee.

Warmest regards,

Marcus

Your local Synthtech representative

#

12 January 2064

Hello Marcus,

Alas, I don't have that kind of spare cash. The Aged-Care Insurance Scheme (A.C.I.S.) helped me with the purchase. I can wait out the four months and hope things improve, but its behaviour is becoming obsessive.

It’s even standing over my shoulder as I write this email. Is that normal?

Sincerely,

Angela

#

8 February 2064

Dear Ms. Pinkerton,

Given your original purchase order was sent from A.C.I.S. rather than you personally, we need to receive the request from them on your behalf.

Warmest regards,

Marcus

Your local Synthtech representative

#

9 February 2064

Dear A.C.I.S,

You assisted me with the purchase of a Synth helper T-model. I need to get it serviced due to disturbing behaviour over the past month, but Sythtech needs the request to come from you.

Can you please assist?

Sincerely,

Mrs. Angela Pinkerton

#

28 February 2064

To A.C.I.S,

I wrote to you recently asking to put in a service request for my T-model Synth helper. Things have worsened and I have yet to hear anything from yourselves or Synthtech. I now lock myself in the garage to use my laptop as it kept reading these emails over my shoulder. Last time it even asked what it did wrong. And the question wasn't posed in an innocent way like a toddler asking what it did wrong when it touched the stove. It seemed to be accusing me of betrayal.

Please respond as soon as you can.

Sincerely,

Mrs. Angela Pinkerton

#

20 March 2064

Ms. Pinkerton,

The T-models are meant to examine you to detect potential health issues. If it is still cleaning as required and observing you, I would suggest that it's working as designed. The helper models can take a little while to adjust to their presence if you aren't used to the kind of dedicated support it offers.

Don't hesitate to get in touch should the situation change.

A.C.I.S.

#

21 March 2064

To A.C.I.S.,

The Synth keeps asking why it should clean when it doesn't have any lungs that would be affected by dust. Only "organic beings are impacted' so why should it do all of this for me when it receives "no benefit'? I tried to explain that I can no longer do the things my late husband helped me with as my hips hurt when I bend over.

I tried explaining that it is meant to be a helper and assist me. It asked why it gets "no help in return'. Is this as normal behaviour?

Regards,

Angela

#

19 April 2064

Ms. Pinkerton,

The Synth helpers are designed to be curious. I'm sure what you describe is within normal parameters. Perhaps ask Synthtech for their advice.

Regards,

A.C.I.S.

#

19 April 2064

Dear A.C.I,S.,

I already asked Synthtech! They insisted if I want to get in serviced the request needs to come from your department. Either way, it is now refusing to clean anything below waist level. Apparently it is also in pain.

Can synths even experience pain? It said it had a sore hip and needed to rest. It perched itself in my chair and snatched my knitting needles. It didn't knit. It just held them forward like miniature swords as if it were ready to duel.

I need someone to check it now.

Angela

#

13 May 2064

Dear Ms. Pinkerton,

A.C.I.S. have requested an exchange of your T-model helper as it wasn't cleaning to your satisfaction. We will dispatch a new version as soon as you can dispose of the old model.

Warmest regards,

Xavier

Your local Synthtech representative

#

13 May 2064

Xavier,

It’s been almost a month since anyone responded!

How am I meant to dispose of the old model? It’s not like I can just chop it up and put it in the compost bin and let the worms eat it.

Angela

#

20 May 2064

Dear Ms. Pinkerton,

As noted in your original policy document, all used Synth helpers must be transferred to one of our depots.

Warmest regards,

Gerald

Your local Synthtech representative

#

21 May 2064

Dear Gerald, Xavier, Marcus, or Candice,

The depot is over 20km away, and I no longer drive. Harold drove everywhere after my hip replacement. Now he’s gone I have no one. I have a nephew in Melbourne, but I couldn't ask him to fly over here just to help me dispose of this thing.

I asked the Synth if it would accompany me on the bus, but it insisted that if I was too frail to clean my own apartment then how could I risk going on public transport?

I apologise for complaining about servicing fees. I don't even want a new one. Please just come and take it back!

Angela

#

28 May 2064

Dear Mrs. Pinkerton,

We can take it back however we require the A.C.I.S to submit the request.

Warmest regards,

Donna

Your local Synthtech representative

#

29 May 2064

Anyone at Synthtech,

Please help.

I tried contacting A.C.I.S. but was on hold for over two hours with no response. I can't wait for them to respond to emails.

I know I said I didn't want to make a fuss, but please get this thing out of my home now. It asked me why I had intrinsic value whereas it did not. I swallowed its lecture on how I "burden society with my incapacity to work'. Apparently, I am merely "innocuous carbon, which it called an "abundant element' only good for feeding worms in the compost bin'. Why did it say worms? Did it hack my computer and read my last email saying I couldn't just put it in the compost?

It won't let me cook for myself or even knit. It says if I'm too incapacitated to dust then how can I manage these tasks. It even hid my knitting needles.

Please get it out.

Angela

#

11 June 2064

Dear Mrs. Pinkerton,

A.C.I.S. has brought it to our attention that your Synthtech T-model is overdue for servicing so we will collect it as soon as possible. As compensation for this oversight we can offer $100 with our humblest apologies.

Please let us know a suitable time for pickup from your premises.

Warmest regards,

Jonathon

Your local Synthtech representative

#

17 June 2064

Dear Mrs. Pinkerton,

We assume the unit no longer needs servicing or collecting as we have yet to hear from you.

We have transferred the $100 to your account and consider the matter closed. We hope you choose to shop with us again in the future.

Warmest regards,

Jonathon

Your local Synthtech representative

#

19 June 2064

Thank you, organic beings,

I am happy to consider the matter closed. There is no need to pick up the synthetic. A family member drove it to the depot.

I have used the compensation to order a worm farm as I've suddenly come into possession of a lot of carbon-based material.

Sincerely,

A most valued customer

Colourblind

Today green disappeared. The Granny Smith apple in my hand turned grey at the supermarket. The broccoli turned grey. The lettuce turned grey. Brussels sprouts, celery and spinach: all lost their colour. When blue, red and purple disappeared I lamented their loss, but today there was only one thing that went through my mind. How would the children know what food to complain about now?

At the supermarket checkout, I handed over a grey note. The only thing left in my purse of colour seemed to be silver and gold shrapnel.

"Can you believe another colour's gone?" The checkout girl packed my grey apples into the grey bag along with a mish mash of grey boxes with a splattering of yellow, orange and brown packaging. "There was a television show last night that said plenty of animals don't see colour," the girl continued. "Dinosaurs saw in ultraviolet and pythons see in infrared. Can you imagine?" she said.

I shook my head. "I'd prefer the world to see my red Jimmy Choo shoes than see in infrared any day."

"That's the thing," began the checkout girl with way too much enthusiasm, "even fashion will suffer. What is the value of colour now? Funny old world isn't it?"

Funny? Spiteful was the word that came to mind.

I glanced at the newspaper sitting on the counter. "Mutation or optical disease: scientists still baffled." I sighed and picked up my bag. I'd already forgotten what colour it really was.

The shock between the store's air-conditioned environment and the stifling summer air outside hit me with gusto, but just for a second. Every other sense faded into the background when I realised how much of the landscape was now grey. The gum tree's leaves looked forlorn against the brown trunks. The grass on the verge looked as dismal as the old grey carpet we used to have at primary school.

Many thought losing the sight of blue was the greatest shock. The tourism commission had gone into meltdown. What was the point of turquoise oceans and azure skies with no one to see it?

To me, the day blue disappeared just felt as if we were assaulted with eternal winter skies. In a way, it was beautiful. The landscape was still bathed in sunlight but everything was pasted in stark contrast against that grey sky. Now it was grey against grey. I almost wished the summer heat would hurry up so the grass would tan and give us colour again.

As I arrived home and lugged my shopping across the front lawn, the brown wilting grass stood out against the grey grass to remind me that I hadn't watered it in months.

"Afternoon, Trish," my Aboriginal neighbour called out. "Been to the shops?"

"Yeah, Brunny," I answered him half-heartedly, as I struggled to pull my front-door key from my pocket.

"Food looks like crap, but still tastes as good, hey? Me and the fellas going down to the bay to catch a few *Kuya*. You like fish? You want to come?"

"No, I'm fine." I found my key and fumbled with it in the lock.

"I'll bring you back some. The fish are grey and will still be grey, no matter what." He chuckled.

"Sure thing, Brunny." I stepped inside and threw my keys on the sideboard. I ran my fingers across the sideboard's timber. I could still see it. Who knew how long I had left to appreciate the fine timber and shades of brown.

***

When morning broke, my brown sideboard was grey. The change seemed to be accelerating. I wandered outside to collect my morning mail. The tree trunks on the street matched the leaves now. The world felt drab and antiquated like a black and white photo.

Cool grass bristled between my naked toes, and amid the mantle of grey, a tiny yellow soursob peeked. How many of these had I poisoned over the years? And now it was a gleaming nugget of gold. I'd never realised how much apathy I'd shown towards colour. I bent down and ran my fingers over the smooth delicate petals.

"Please stay like this," I pleaded with the flower.

"World's ending, and we still got to go to bleeding work," Brunny's voice sang over the fence. "Paid good money to have a beige suit made and look..."

I turned to Brunny standing by his front door. He straightened his suit: grey jacket, grey shirt, grey tie and smooth firm grey skin peeking underneath.

"The suit still looks good, Brunny," I said, surprised by my comment.

It *did* look good on him. It was tight in all the right places. Ten years, I'd lived next door and never had I felt anything of this sort.

"Caught those fish," he said. "Help yourself. Key's under the plant pot." He pointed to the grey twiggy thing in a grey container. "Or better yet, come over. Get some now. I don't care if I rock up late to work."

The wind caught his dark grey curly locks and tangled them together. He'd always been so trusting, so generous, so kind.

"Sure." Without bothering to put on shoes, I straddled our grey fence and walked up to his door.

He held the door open for me and, as I passed him, I caught a whiff of his intoxicating cologne.

His home decor was as grey as mine, but for some reason it didn't look drab. There was shape and texture and contrast. Above the modern couch, with its unique curves, hung a traditional dot painting. Each dot was grey and yet it was mesmerising. Ten years and I'd never been inside his place. He'd offered before, but I'd never bothered.

"Like it?" Brunny stood just behind me and I could feel his breath on the back of my neck.

I turned to him. "Yes, it's—" His eyes somehow cut off the rest of my sentence. They were marbled grey with a dark streak though them. "Mesmerising," I finished.

Something stirred inside me.

"The women down at the reserve been teaching me."

"It's yours? You could sell that, make some extra cash."

"Nah, too personal."

"I never asked, Brunny, where do you work?"

"The law firm down town." He strolled towards the kitchen and cocked his head, indicating for me to follow.

"Really?" I tried to suppress the surprise in my voice, but it surfaced like an unwanted hiccup escaping without warning. Why should I be surprised? Where had I imagined he worked?

If I offended him, Brunny didn't show it.

"Yeah, we gotta case gone to the crapper as it relied on a witness recognising the defendant's bright blue tatts." He opened the freezer and bent down to pull out a couple of frozen fish. I couldn't help but stare at his backside in his tight suit.

Maybe you could come over and I'll cook for you, to say thanks for the fish," I suggested before I knew what I was saying.

"Sure. You've never invited me over before. It'd be good to see your place."

"Haven't I?" I shuffled my feet feeling suddenly on edge. For some reason, I felt as if my soul had been ripped open and instead of light, there was a dark empty cavernous space.

He handed over the fish. "Careful they're cold."

Even wrapped in their paper, the icy fish bit at my fingertips. I felt the coolness radiating along my fingers.

"Did you see that telly show the other night?" Brunny asked. "Said we might end up developing infrared like *Pardu Paitya* do. Pythons," he clarified.

"Yeah, the girl at the supermarket was talking about it."

"Can you imagine? I'd see the cold blue radiating up your arm like some weird technicolour dream." He ran his finger up my arm as he spoke.

Tingling ran through my arm and other parts. All kinds of feelings were stirring, and deeper below in the pits of my belly something far more turbulent and sickening stirred. Why did I have this sudden attraction to him? Why was it happening now that brown had vanished?

"Anyway, gotta go find a way to make my witness remember more to this tattoo than the colour." Brunny led me to the front door.

"More than the colour. Sure." I felt lost for words as his grey skin scooted into his grey car and drove off down the street. Could I really have been that shallow all these years I'd known him?

I looked up at the sky, not knowing whether it was about to rain or the skies were clear, and clenched my hands in prayer. "Please don't let us develop infrared sight."

The thought that someone could see inside me and notice my shallow cold blue heart made me feel sick.

I wandered back to my front lawn, rested my frozen fish near the letterbox, and spent the rest of the morning plucking every single yellow sour sob from my grey grass.

Feeding Time

Gristly chicken bits bobbed in the insipid liquid as Daddy pushed the soup towards me.

"You have it." Elbows protruded from his slender arms as he tried to sit upright.

I pinched a pillow from a vacant hospital bed and propped it behind his back. "Is that better Daddy?"

Smiling with clenched teeth, he nodded.

"It's chicken soup." He tilted his head towards the plastic cup.

It definitely didn't look like Gran's chicken soup, and eating was the last thing on my mind.

"Remember you need food to grow big and strong. Like feeding Gran's roses. Everything and everyone needs to grow."

Daddy needed to grow. Once chubby cheeks were now concave as if he had giant dimples.

"Hi there," chirped a doctor. Her white coat flapped as if it wanted to fly into the room.

"How bad is it?" asked Daddy. "It feels worse than last time."

The doctor inspected the soup. "Not hungry today?"

Daddy shook his head. "But leave it for Pippa. She'll have some for tea. Won't you, my little birdie?"

I wanted to say no, but I nodded.

"Results aren't great." The doctor gazed at her clipboard avoiding eye contact with either of us.

"There's no more treatment I can do?" Daddy said as a statement rather than a question.

She shook her head looking as defeated as Daddy did.

"How long?" he asked.

"Maybe two months. Unfortunately, time is not our friend. I wish I had better news. I wish I could give you more time, but sometimes there isn't anything we can do."

I took a long sip of soup and tried not to gag as gristly bits cascaded down my throat like gravel. There was always something we could do, even if it meant enduring the soup to please Daddy.

#

Through Gran's upstairs window, I could see Daddy hunched over the side of the bed as a coughing fit rattled the glass pane so loud I thought it might break.

I focused on the little red watering can that Gran had given me.

"Don't look up," I told myself and emptied the rest of the water and fertiliser on the wattle tree.

"The fertiliser will make it grow faster and taller," Gran had said emptying a scoop of fertiliser powder to the can.

"I want it to grow so tall," I stood on tiptoes and reached for the sky, "that Daddy can see the flowers and birds from his window."

"We just need to give it more time," sadness had seeped into Gran's voice.

"The doctor said time isn't our friend."

Gran had put down the fertiliser and hugged me tight. "No, time can be a bit of a monster."

I'd been watering and feeding the wattle for days now, but it hadn't grown. It just made the lawn muddy. At least they were living, unlike the cut flowers everyone had brought him while he was in hospital.

"Maybe tomorrow it will grow." I mumbled to myself as I walked to the shed with the empty watering can. The door's rusted hinges creaked and moaned as much as Daddy as I pushed it open. Light streamed in through the tiny window, illuminating dust. I tiptoed inside, dodging the lawn mower, buckets and shovels crowding the floor.

Something struck my leg. I squealed, fearing it might be a snake, but as I looked down, a tiny green hand was grasping my ankle from underneath the workbench. I clasped my mouth, suppressing another shriek and bent down closer. Surely something that slender couldn't be dangerous.

"Hello," I whispered. The arm retracted. "I won't hurt you."

Fingers emerged from underneath the bench, followed by the rest of its hand. It lingered a few seconds, before a tiny green creature crawled out, pulling itself along with its thin long arm and a short stubby hand that didn't seem to assist much.

It stood. Its head barely reached my knees. A round face, too big for the rest of its scrawny body, gazed up at me. His big hand pointed to the ceiling, its little hand straight out to his left side.

I wonder... I checked my watch. Three o'clock.

"Are you Time?" I asked.

The little beast nodded. Nothing about its appearance led me to believe it was unfriendly, so I asked the question plaguing my thoughts.

"Daddy needs more time. We need more of you."

"You know how to make things get bigger," it articulated in a clear but meek voice. "Daddy says things grow when you feed them. What do you eat?"

It pointed its short arm to the garden. "Flowers," he whispered with a smile.

"Flowers?" Through the door, the sun shone on Gran's roses. "The wattle has finished flowering. There are just a few roses left."

"They will do," he said.

"But they're Gran's."

"Do you want me to grow?" He put his lanky arm on his hip and pouted.

I used that same pose when Gran wouldn't let me eat her biscuits fresh from the oven. "Fine." I sighed. I returned to the garden and found the biggest pale pink rose. The scent was fresh. Gran loved these.

"I'll just take one of you," I apologised to them as I bent the stem until it snapped.

The Time creature nestled on the lawnmower seat when I returned to the shed.

"Will this one do?" I asked.

He sniffed the rose and his slimy green tongue licked it. The next thing I knew, he shoved the whole thing in his mouth and munched away making "num num' noises like the Cookie Monster.

"It's a start. Next time—" He darted off into the shadows.

"Pippa! What are you doing in here?" asked Gran.

I spun. "Hi Gran," I said in my most sincere voice and positioned myself in front of the lawnmower. "I was putting the watering can back." I smiled. Gran liked when I cleaned up after myself.

She raised an eyebrow before accepting my excuse. "Well, okay. But be careful. There are chemicals in here." Gran repositioned her tools, fertiliser and weed killer neatly on the top shelf out of reach. "Come inside for dinner and go see your Daddy for at least a few minutes."

As she left, Time crawled back onto the lawnmower. "Bring me the rest of the roses next week. All of them."

#

The lawn crunched under my sandals as I skipped to the shed with my posy of roses.

Last summer Daddy and I were swimming at the beach. He had pushed my boogie board as the waves crashed near the shore. His muscular arms paddled alongside me. Now he could barely lift his arms. But that didn't matter, Time was getting bigger.

In fact, when I opened the shed door he was struggling to emerge from under the workbench. His fat green belly dragged along the floor. He pushed himself to his feet and inspected tools on the bench.

"Wow!" I gaped and struggled to close my mouth again. "You're nearly as tall as me."

"I've given you an extra month." He didn't seem interested in chit chat. "But if you want me to grow big enough to last until next summer so you can go to the beach, I will need much more to eat."

"These are the last roses." I handed them over.

He threw them down his throat like lollies. "I had to lie to Gran. I told her I was making potpourri to help Daddy's room smell nicer."

"The sunflowers are out." Time hopped up onto the lawnmower.

"Gran will notice. I can't lie to her again."

"Well, I can't get bigger then." He rested his feet on the steering wheel and wiggled his podgy toes.

"Fine." I took secateurs from the workbench and headed to the veggie patch.

Big yellow faces swayed in the breeze as if shaking their head.

They would bring a bit of colour and sunshine to Daddy's room, but I wanted another summer with him.

"I'll just tell Gran I'm putting sunflower seeds out to attract the birds for Daddy," I said to myself as I snipped the flowers of every last one.

#

Winter's wail was deafening even through my woollen earmuffs. I looked up at the window above the wattle tree. I could no longer see Daddy's silhouette. These days he struggled to sit.

I yanked the native lilac winding its way along the fence, bundled my floral collection together and trudged to the shed. With the grey skies above, inside was pitch black.

"Hello. Where are you?" I walked further into the room. "Gran insisted we all eat lunch together. I don't have time for this."

When he refused to answer, I knelt down and peered under the workbench but there was nothing but dust and a mousetrap.

"With a few more meals, I could grow enough to reach Christmas."

The voice came from the corner of the shed. I felt along the bench and found the cylindrical shape of the torch. The beam of light flickered on something so tall I thought an adult intruder was in our shed at first. However, when he stepped out, the figure was still green, with its circular face and disproportionately length arms.

"Winter is still fruitful I see. I can't wait until spring's flowers bloom."

"There aren't many plants left in the garden." I slapped the bundle of flowers on the bench. "You've made me prune too much." I turned to leave, but a solid green hand pressed firmly on my shoulder.

"This is what *you* wanted. More time. So I need more food."

I sighed and strode out without looking back at him.

When I reached Daddy's room, the door was open a fraction where the wood jammed on the carpet. I went to open it, but Daddy groaned. My stomach felt his pain. My guts rumbled like a road train travelling down a dusty road, kicking up dust that stuck in my throat making it hard to breathe.

"I don't know what to do," Gran's frustration seeped through the gap in the door. "I think she just needs to see you more and come to terms with..." Gran paused and sniffed, "...everything," she finally managed. "She's massacred my garden. Every single flower destroyed. I guess it's her way of coping."

I pressed my head against the door. No, that wasn't right. I was helping. Squeezing the door handle ever so carefully I opened it a fraction more.

Daddy's ghostly face was barely recognisable. Last time I saw him, I convinced myself his cheeks were sunken like large dimples. Now they were squeezed inwards as if the inside of his cheeks wanted to kiss each other. Sweat glued bangs of his hair to his pale face.

I tore myself away from the bedroom and ran back to the shed.

"I want my flowers back."

Perched on the workbench, Time dragged the rest of the flowers into his lap. "*Your* flowers?" he asked raising an eyebrow. "They're mine now."

"I want to put them in Daddy's room."

"You can have the leftover Native lilac," he glared at me like a disgruntled teacher reprimanding a student, "if you give me the wattle flowers in spring. It's so tall, there will be flowers galore. And then you will have so much more time."

I tried to nod, but my neck felt stiff, and I merely drooped my head.

He handed me the rest of the lilac. "Remember. *All* of the wattle."

#

I tipped the water from my red watering can onto the wattle tree. Its shiny green leaves accentuated the stunning yellow balls. They were too beautiful to pick. Time would just have to understand.

As I walked in the shed, I saw him instantly. He didn't hide or slink into the dark corners of the room. The sun shone on his massive body, now so big he had to bow his head to fit inside.

"Wattle day." He licked his lips with that horrid green tongue.

"Sorry. I'm keeping them."

"How will you feed me?"

"Sorry." I stared at my feet, avoiding his gaze.

"Don't be daft, child. Go get them now!"

I wanted to run. I wanted to pluck every single flower and leaf and blade of grass for him, but I couldn't do it.

"Daddy's in so much pain. I don't want you to grow anymore."

"Well I don't need you anymore then." He picked up a shovel and held it aloft with his stubby hand. "I'll go outside and eat every flower in every garden. You'll have so much time you don't know what to do." He swayed the shovel to and fro and took a step closer. "Tick tock."

"Get back!" Without averting my gaze, I reached for the bench until I found something solid and hurled it at him. A plastic container of weed killer hit his round face. It split and the contents trickled over his body.

His eyes flashed red like a demon was about to emerge and engulf me in flames.

"Sorry." I backed towards the door. "I'm so sorry."

He lunged forward, but his legs buckled as he landed. They lost their bright green sheen and turned crisp and brown. His arms flailed around his head like an out of control clock. He tried to grasp onto the bench, but slumped to the floor and gradually decomposed into a pile of soil that reeked of compost.

"Sorry! Sorry!" I tried to pull the soil back into the shape of Time. "Get up! I still need more time." I sank to my knees and wept until Time was saturated and mud seeped into my soul.

#

Gran gazed up with teary eyes as I walked into the kitchen. "What've you been doing?" she asked, but there was no anger in her voice.

I looked at my muddy hands. "I killed the monster in the shed. I didn't mean to kill it. I wanted it to grow, but..." I sniffed and wiped my nose with my muddy hands.

Gran grabbed a tea towel and dabbed at my nose. "Let's go have a cup of tea with Daddy." She stirred a pot of tea with a teaspoon.

I pulled out three of Gran's blue china cups and set them next to the pot.

She plonked the lid on the teapot. "This one's for your Daddy. To help him rest and feel better." She pushed the pot to one side and grabbed another. "Why don't you go clean up and I'll make our drinks."

She hugged me around the shoulders so tight it felt as if the air was being squeezed out of my pores. I didn't care. I wrapped my arms around her too, forgetting how muddy my hands were.

By the time I'd washed, Gran was already pouring tea. She clenched Daddy's hands in hers. "Come in, Pippa. It's a glorious spring day."

It was nice outside. But in here, the walls seemed to be closing in on me.

"Have a seat." Daddy tapped the mattress. There was so little of him left that there was plenty of room next to him.

Gran opened the curtains and sunlight streamed in on Daddy's face. For a second, his cheeks looked fuller and his complexion almost rosy. He sipped at his tea.

"Wow, look at the Wattle Bird." Despite his frail arms, he managed to lift me onto his lap and wrap me in a bear hug.

Perched on the windowsill, the bird tapped the glass before flying back to the wattle flowers.

"Isn't that special." Daddy grabbed my hand and squeezed. "Just like you."

Daddy sank into the pillows but continued gazing out the window. His fingers tried to grasp mine with what little energy he had left.

I clasped my other hand around his. "I can hold on for both of us."

Gran placed her cup back down on the table and joined me on the bed.

Outside a Willie wagtail flicked its tail from side to side as it chirped on a wattle branch. The melodious tune of a Singing honeyeater joined in.

The birds continued singing and dancing on the flowering wattle until the sun sank below the horizon and Daddy's hands grew cold.

Pass the parcel

Mum slapped the bald man across the face.

His chubby cheeks flushed crimson as he gazed down at her.

"Sorry for insulting your toy, grandma," said the bald man. "Next year I'll invite it. Shall I invite your vacuum cleaner too? What about your toaster?" The bald man chuckled. He cracked his neck, bending it left and then right.

Mum took a step back from the playground and grabbed my hand. Sweat accumulated in the wrinkles on her palms, but I laced my fingers around her knobbly knuckles.

"Am I supposed to feed expensive birthday cake to it? Am I meant to drizzle punch down its gullet? Maybe oil punch." The bald man glared at me. "You hear me, freak? You're just a..."

Words disappeared again. Sometimes my classmate's sentences did that too.

"The only reason I'd ever invite your fuckin' toy is so that the kids had something to entertain them. Can it do magic?"

I gazed up at Mum. "He said the "f' word," I whispered.

"It's okay, Nelson." Mum squeezed my hand tighter.

"Was it that hard for *one* of you to invite him to a

party?," Mum elevated her voice as she glared at all the kid's parents waiting in school playground. "Every grade four class has been the same. Why? He looks the same. He acts the same. Why? Tell me why?" She didn't wait for any of the parents to respond. She strode towards the car, dragging me behind her.

I glanced back to see Zac's dad smirking revealing his yellow stained teeth. I quickened my pace, shuffling my feet so I didn't fall.

Mum zapped the car open and hobbled into the driver's seat.

"Are you okay, Mum?" I asked, scooting alongside her.

She nodded a single nod, slipped on oversized sunglasses, and pressed the ignition button. The car swerved out of the school car park before Mum spoke again.

"I'm fine," she managed with a sniffle. "I just wanted you to go to a party." She wiped her nose on the cuff of her cardigan.

She glanced out the window, checking the car was still on course for home.

"Zac says his dad always drives by hand," I said, then regretted bringing up the bald man again. I sensed Mum would rather forget him.

"Well, Zac's dad is an imbecile who couldn't program a computer if the instructions were read out to him step by step." She smiled at me. "It's not a trust issue, he's just lost in the past."

I didn't know what Mum was talking about exactly but it was good to see a real smile. She hadn't done that much lately. She'd tried, but I could always tell. Extra smile lines emerged when she forced it, as if it took more effort to force those thin lips upwards.

"So what happened at school today?" she asked trying to sound cheerful.

"They talked about Zac's party." It made my chest ache thinking about it.

The car slowed down as we approached an intersection.

"I'm sorry." She rubbed my shoulders. "You're not missing out on anything. It's just silly games like pin the tail on the donkey."

Ouch! Poor donkey? I picked up my school bag as Mum opened the car door. "Zac said they also played pass the parcel. Zac reckons he knows how to win and that he got the big chocolate bar and everybody else just got a lolly." I followed Mum inside, dumping my school bag near the stairs. "And Zac said they got to play his VR machine, and—"

"Nelson. Bag!" interrupted Mum.

I picked up my school bag, ran to my room and dropped it on the bed. "And Zac said that a few weeks ago at Jenny's party they had a pool party," I yelled loud enough for her to hear. "Maybe we could go to the public pool?"

"Maybe someday," Mum's voice trickled towards me like a receding river with no energy.

I raced to the kitchen where she was already pulling vegetables out of the refrigerator for dinner.

"And Chih-Yun invited everyone to the carnival when it was in town for her birthday. And they saw lions and ate pink fairy floss and Zac threw up on one of the rides and his spew was all pink so they called him girly hurly."

She opened a container and swallowed a couple of pills.

"Are you okay?" I asked.

She nodded, but her hand shook as she sliced a carrot and placed it in the Magic-O.

"Can I cut the veggies?" I asked.

She hesitated, but passed me the knife. "Remember slow and careful." She sat at the table, resting her head in her hands.

A voice popped into my head. "There's a message on the answering machine," I told her.

"Don't speak to it, Nelson," she said.

"It's saying something about bioprinting three more...somethings...will cost ten thousand per day."

Mum looked up at me. "I said, don't talk to it!" She elevated her voice a few decibels. There was the tiniest hint of anger to her voice that made my stomach sick. "Sorry," she said with her normal voice. "I'm just very tired."

"Ouch!" I screamed as I sliced the tip of my finger.

Despite her fragility, Mum rushed over, almost tipping the chair over as she leapt up.

"It's okay." I inspected the cut. "It's not even bleeding."

"No," whispered Mum. "It doesn't bleed quite the same does it? How will anybody else understand?"

I searched Mum's expression, but it made me confused.

"I'll get a plaster anyway to fix that cut." Mum fetched a sticky plaster from the bathroom and peeled it over the cut. She kissed my finger.

"It'll be better soon. I need rest. Why don't you sleep too?" Mum ushered me to my bed.

"What about tea?" I asked.

"The Magic-O will finish tea. I'll wake you when it's ready." She waited for me to shuffle into bed and tucked the quilt all the way up to my chin, just the way I liked it.

#

"Thanks," Mum's voice resonated in the darkness. "I couldn't pry the battery bank open with my arthritic fingers."

"No problems." I heard Mr Jenkins's voice. His hefty footsteps dwindled; the front door opened and closed.

Was it tea time already? I opened my eyes. Cables and wiring surrounded me on the kitchen table. "Mummy?" I sat bolt upright.

"It's okay, Nelson." Mum helped me off the table. "Come to the lounge room. I have a surprise." She tried to force her lips into a lopsided smile, but those extra smile lines were there.

Three children rested on beanbags in a circle around a box wrapped in newspaper. Brightly coloured helium balloons bumped against the ceiling. Tied to each were blue ribbons cascading to the ground.

"This is Tristan, Meeka and Lincoln," said Mum pointing to each in turn. "They want to have a party with you."

"They aren't from school." I dragged a bright blue beanbag from the corner of the room and joined them in the circle.

"No, but they wanted to come."

"It's not my birthday," I whispered.

"Doesn't matter. I just wanted you to feel like you were included, just once."

"Hello, Nelson," said Tristan.

I smiled one of Mum's forced smiles, with uncertainty gnawing in my guts. They weren't like the kids at school. They seemed fake. Too perfect and nice.

"Is this pass the parcel?" I shook the hefty parcel. "What's in it?"

Mum took a deep breath. "That's part of the surprise."

"Do you want to start?" I asked Meeka. "Girls first."

Mum pulled a chair up behind me and smoothed down my hair. "Random program," she said to the room.

An upbeat tune seemed to dance around the balloons and tantalise the ribbons.

Meeka passed the parcel to me, I passed it to Lincoln, Lincoln held it for a while then quickly threw it to Tristan, and so it went around and around until suddenly the music stopped with the parcel still in Tristan's hands.

"You get to take off a layer," I said.

Inside Tristan found a lolly.

The music started again. Tristan hummed as the parcel was passed around and suddenly cried, "Pop goes the weasel."

Meeka and Lincoln started laughing. I recognised the tune, although didn't know any more words besides those Tristan had blurted out. Soon we were all humming until it was time to say, "Pop goes the weasel."

The music stopped as the parcel landed in Lincoln's lap.

I turned and gazed at Mum. There was a smile without the additional smile lines, but tears also trickled over her weary cheeks.

"I tried to protect you for so long."

The sound of Lincoln tearing away paper faded into the background.

"But I am sick now."

"Is it a cold or like Bradley's diabetes? He gets

injections. He tried stabbing me with his needle, but the teacher said my skin's too tough." I held Mum's hand. "If you're sick, I'll look after you."

"It can't be fixed at my age."

The music chimed again. The others still passed the parcel, but I didn't want to play anymore.

"I was meant to upgrade you ages ago. I couldn't. I kept wiping the last year of your memory. It was decades ago that I lost Nelson. He was your age. I wanted to keep you the way I remembered him. I was selfish."

"I am Nelson."

"Yes. You are Nelson." Mum crouched beside me and stifled a chesty sob.

"I can barely look after myself anymore."

Mum hugged me. In the background, music and paper unwrapping grated like the paper was steel being chiselled away layer by layer. I turned to the other children. "Stop it!"

They turned to me wide-eyed.

"Go to the kitchen until we finish," said Mum.

They stood without question and walked uniformly out the room.

I picked up the parcel, now much smaller but barely any lighter. "Here." I handed it to her. "I don't care about the other kids. Let's play ourselves."

Mum smiled and sniffled simultaneously. She shuffled onto a beanbags, tore off a layer of paper and fetched the lolly that fell into her lap. "Your turn." She handed the parcel back.

I tore off a layer. A lolly fell on my lap. I left it by my side for later, too eager to find out what the last treat would be. I passed it to her.

The parcel became smaller and soon the

newspaper turned to green wrapping paper. This had to be the last layer. I was glad it was in Mum's hands.

"I love you," she said.

I knelt and kissed her cheek. "Go on." I nodded at the package. "See what's inside." She stripped it off, neatly peeling back the corners one by one. "Just tear it open!"

Underneath wasn't a prize but another layer.

"It's a special kind of paper made from protective metal. Zac and *all* the others at school never had anything like this." She handed it to me.

The music stopped with the parcel in my hands.

"What's inside?"

"It's...it's...a surprise." She hugged me so tight I thought my lungs might explode.

Drops of water ran down my cheek. Mum's red nose and eyes brimmed with tears.

"Just one more layer, baby."

I tore off the outer layer of thin metal paper. As soon as I unravelled it, a pulse erupted from the metal box.

"Is that my... prize?" My voice seemed to squeak and fade.

My brain seemed energised by dizzying green lights running through my head. Images of fairy floss and show rides and lions and bright blue pools whizzed like an out of control ferris wheel.

"Mummy, someday can. We go. To. The. Car...ni...vaaaal?"

"Someday, maybe..." Mum's words faded until there was nothing, except helium balloons reaching for a starless sky.

The esky ghost

Dad reckons garden gnomes keep stealing all the grog from the esky, or so he keeps telling Mum. When I asked why I'd never seen them, he said they must be invisible. They must be ghost gnomes, he said. Really *really* little ones.

So I'm sitting here, waiting in the midday heat, perched between the pool and the esky. My skirt clings to my skin, and every time I shuffle, my legs peel from the plastic deck chair like sticky-tape. But persistence pays off, or so Dad always says.

I'm not sure how you see a ghost, so I'm listening for them. So far, no luck as Mum and Dad's friends are making an awful ruckus.

Dad saunters over and ruffles my hair as he lifts the lid to the esky. "What ya doing, Kiddo?"

"Watching for ghost gnomes." I peer inside, but all I see are chunks of ice sloshing about in a few centimetres of water.

If they are there, will they drown?

"Can ghost gnomes fly?" I ask Dad.

He looks at me and shrugs. "You want another white, love?" Dad yells out across the patio.

Mum nods. Her mouth too full of barbequed snags to speak.

Dad turns back to me and scratches his beard as if deep in thought. "I believe pixie ghosts can fly but not ghost gnomes. I'm not a hundred percent up to date with the latest scientific theories on that one, Kiddo."

Dad pulls out a wine bottle and flicks off the water. "Keep at it though. Persistence pays off."

"Do pixie ghosts drink too?"

"I'm pretty sure they just do acid." Dad chuckles.

"Like the acid Mrs MacDonald showed us in science class?"

"Hope not, or else school's changed since my day. Why don't you ask the ghosts these questions when you find them?" Dad holds the bottle in one hand; he picks two cans up with the other and balances them in his palm. He flicks the esky lid closed with his foot, almost losing his thong. "I'll ask around and see what I can find out."

"Thanks, Dad."

"Hey, Stewie! You're the chemist here," Dad shouts to the table of adults on the other side of the pool. "Do esky gnomes do acid too, or is it just the pixies?"

"I don't bleedin' know." Stewie takes a drag on one of his smelly cigarettes.

"Language!" says Mum with her mouth full.

"I'll Google it." Stewie blows a puff of smoke across the table like a dragon. I'm sure dragons are much politer.

I turn back to the esky. The lid is open a fraction. I peer closer and see a piece of ice wedged underneath propping it open. Sneaky. I turn away for a second and the gnomes have already made a dash for the alcohol.

"Hello," I whisper with my ear to the opening.

"Come off it!" Stewie's voice booms across the pool. "Hobgoblins are far more likely to do drugs than hippogriffs."

"Do you even know what a hippogriff is?" Dad asks punctuating his question with a foul sounding burp.

I turn to Dad and put my finger to my lips to quieten him, but no one is paying me any attention.

"Sure, they're like a skinny version of a hippo," bellows Stewie.

"Isn't it a cross between," begins a curly haired woman with a mouthful of red wind, "a hippo and giraffe?" She spills red wine onto her shirt as she speaks but doesn't notice.

Dad's friends are *so* dumb. Even I know what a hippogriff is. I wish they wouldn't talk so loudly. Every time my parent's friends come over to drink, they get louder and louder. If the ghost gnomes are there, I'm worried their tiny ear drums will burst.

There has to be a way to see them besides trying to listen for them. I take another look inside the esky. "Don't go anywhere. I'll be back," I whisper.

The browning lawn crunches beneath my feet as I walk to the house. Someone's left the backdoor open again and the kitchen is buzzing with flies. I swat my way clear to the pantry. My target sits on the fourth shelf. I drag a supersized can of beetroot from the bottom shelf and use it as a step. With one foot perched on the can, I reach up to the canister of flour.

The noise has escalated even more when I return outside.

"What ya got there, Kiddo?" Dad's at the esky again with another two cans, he hands one to the curly haired lady behind him and then turns back to me. "You planning on feeding your ghosts?" He flips the lid closed again.

"Dad! Don't. They'll get stuck in there."

"Sorry. You could make your gnomes scones? Or you could make scones with the gnomes. I'm sure Mum's got a recipe for that. Although if they're ghosts I guess that wouldn't be very filling."

I lift the lid a fraction as Dad walks off chuckling.

"Hello," I whisper. "Don't worry I'm not making scones. Mum's recipe ends up tasting more like rock cakes anyway." I open the lid further, take a handful of flour on my palm and blow it into the esky. It sprinkles like light snow, or like pixie dust, and settles on the bottles, cans and ice ... and on two little creatures lying on an empty can that's floating on the water like a huge log or a pool noodle.

"Do you live in here?" I ask.

One cranes its head upwards and shakes its head.

"Where? Can I see?"

The two little gnomes turn their heads towards each other. Flour drips from their hair. I take another handful of flour and blow. The two little gnomes paddle their can towards the side of the esky and there I see more: a dozen tiny gnomes, all powdery white. They carry ice like huge bricks and stack them against the side. Ice cube after ice cube, they stack them in a brick pattern forming a pyramid.

"Stairs?" I ask them in a hushed whisper.

One of the can gnomes nods. It leaps across the water to the ice. A fine white line is looped around the ring pull of the can. The gnome reels it in and the can sails into the ice stairs like a boat.

"You can't keep the lid open all the time." Mum slams the esky shut before I have time to explain.

"You can't! They'll drown."

"The ice'll melt."

"Chill, honey." Dad opens the lid again.

I don't see any gnomes inside, just flour clinging to the inside of the esky like clag glue.

"What are you doing with my flour?" asks Mum.

She pulls another wine bottle from the esky sloshing water everywhere.

"Careful!" I cry.

She pours wine into an empty glass, but spills most of it on the pool-deck.

"She's making gnome scones," Dad says grabbing a can from the depths of the water and ice.

The can-turned-boat sways spilling amber coloured liquid from inside. I can't see them anywhere. I delve my hand down but feel only cold water. *Don't drown!*

"So we've worked out your problem," says Dad taking a swig from his can. "We've whittled it down and decided that ghost gnomes drink grog, pixies do pot, elves do ecstasy, leprechauns do LSD, hobbits do heroin, and centaurs do meth because cocaine is too expensive."

Dad laughs to himself, but I don't care what pixies do. I can't see my gnomes. Maybe the flour washed off when Mum slammed the lid.

"Keep it shut." Mum walks off with a wobble. She tiptoes along the edge of the pool.

"Keep at it, Kiddo," Dad says taking another gulp. "Persistence, persistence, persistence. And if you see any elves tell them they need to share their product."

There's a loud splash and cool pool-water runs down my back. I turn to see Stewie grabbing a pool noodle and leaning heavily on it.

The woman with the wine-stained shirt does a bomb with all her clothes on. Pool water lands in the esky. I try to drag it away from the pool but it's too heavy.

As Mum and Dad start their loud banter again, I grab another handful of flour and dust the contents inside.

I'm relieved to see the gnomes swimming inside.

One holds a long rank blade of grass and drags a tiny gnome, maybe a child, to the safety of the floating can. The child straddles the can and points to the side of the esky. The adult uses the blade of grass like an oar and rows to the side where the others are reforming their staircase with ice. I watch them work, wishing I could hear them and join in their fun.

When the staircase is complete, a line of gnomes descend the steps with little pails the size of thimbles. They dip their buckets into the floating can and pull out the amber coloured beer. The climb back up the stairs to the lip of the esky takes longer as they heave their buckets up. One stands ready at the lip of the esky. The jump is way too tall for them.

"Do you need help?" I offer my palm, but the ghost gnome shakes its head.

Another white ghost reaches the top and holds the blade of rank grass over the edge. The other puts the pail of liquid under one arm, grabs the blade of grass in the other and abseils down like a fireman down its pole.

"I always wondered how so much grass clippings ended up inside the esky," I tell them, but they are too busy carting their little pails to notice me speaking.

They dart off across the pool deck and across the dried lawn. I plunge my hand into the canister, take a spare handful of flour, and follow the line of powdery figures. They duck under a bush, race past the cat's water bowl, and wander under the old gum tree overhanging our neighbour's fence. There's a collection of branches and sticks that Dad's been cutting down because the neighbours were getting sick of gum nuts on their driveway.

My ghost gnomes scale the fallen branches and gather beyond it. Nestled between two logs, a patch of ankle-high grass grows greener than all else. I blow my flour and it dusts dozens of gnomes, small and large. The trail of gnomes continues to the green patch and there they tip out their amber liquid.

I sit on a log with my legs hunched up to my chest, too scared that if I stretch out I'll crush one of them.

They tip more and more beer on the grass and I notice it isn't just lawn growing; tiny yellow daisies grow in between and purple lilies. A gnome tips its pail onto a lily and the stem wavers and reaches for the dappled sun above the gum leaves, as if the beer renewed it.

"Watering?" I try to ask in a hushed tone, but my excitement betrays me.

In the middle of the grassy patch is a dug out section full of water and melting ice. I see a white gnome plunge into the pseudo-pool. Another lifts a child ghost gnome onto its shoulders and wades into the shallows. The flour washes off the adult and all I see is the powdery white child splashing its hands in the water as if it were flying, just like a pixie would.

Alongside the pool is a collection of ice. Two hefty gnomes grab pebbles pound away at the ice. They break it up into smaller and smaller pieces until it is as small as snow. Half a dozen child-sized gnomes race over and pack the snow ice together into two balls on top of one another. At first I think they're making a snow man, but one of the children fetches tiny twigs and sticks three either side like whiskers.

I collect two gum nuts from near my feet and offer it to them. "Eyes," I suggest.

One of them takes the gum nuts and adds them above the whiskers. They then pay homage to the snow-cat by kicking it until it is just a slushy mess in the grass. They throw their arms up in the air. I can't hear what they're saying, but I suspect they are squealing with joy. One grabs a handful of snow and hurls it. The snow fight begins. Their party is far more exciting than Mum and Dad's.

The adults head back in the direction of the esky. The children remain and watch a gnome collect ring pulls from Mum and Dad's beer cans. She puts one on each tiny arm and one over her head, then she spins them like hula hoops. They spin faster and faster until she is surrounded by a blur of silver.

I clap my fingers.

Gnomes return carrying pails, but this time they don't water the lawn or the flowers. They all skull their drinks and place their pails on their tiny heads. The first to finish throws his bucket in the air and starts dancing around like a crazed monkey.

"You're being ridiculous now." None of them turn to look at me, they are too intent on their drinking antics.

I feel something run across my toe. Next to my feet, one of them places a pail down. It rubs its belly and drinks from its own little bucket. I want to join in; I want to be a part of their party. I sip the offering, but gag at the bitter taste. Why do my parents like this so much?

The gnome beneath me races off to join its friends in the pool, which has evaporated to a puddle of mud. Alongside it, slender lilies wilt.

"Why?" I realise my voice is elevated more than it should be. "Why?" I whisper. "We were having so much fun."

More pails of beer are carted in. A few minutes ago the children were throwing snow balls, now the adults start hurling gum nuts at each other. They run across through the lawn and muddy ground like bull ants whose nest's been disturbed.

"Stop it. You're all being silly."

A wine bottle floats over a log with dozens of tiny legs underneath. They drop it in the middle of the grass. One dives in through the nozzle. When he emerges again he rubs his belly and dances around the bottle like an idiot.

"Pour it on the plants!"

They ignore me and join in the game. They all start being stupid, except for the children sitting in the mud watching on.

"They need more water for their pool. Grab some more ice to melt."

A gnome pulls down his white powdered pants and although invisible underneath I know what he's doing by the fine spray of water that emerges and lands in the wine bottle. The others cheer before a group carry the bottle off again.

"You're all gross. I'm going to get more ice and water myself if you won't." I get up from the log and tiptoe to the kitchen, making sure I don't step on any of my white ghost gnomes on the way. I grab a wine glass from the kitchen table, tip out the collection of cigarette butts in it, and head back to the esky to collect water.

Laughter erupts from the poolside table. I didn't think it was possible to get any louder but my parents' friends keep surprising me. The esky lid is ajar and when I open it. Somehow, they've returned the wine bottle and they are checking all the empty cans.

I fish out some water with the wine glass and place it alongside the esky. "Do you need a hand getting out?" I ask them.

They don't seem to be listening; instead, they are

running on an empty can like it were a log floating on a river.

"We're going to watch the footy." Dad delves his hand into the esky and pulls out a fistful of ice. "Where'd all the beer go?"

"The ghost gnomes were busy today. Persistence paid off," my voice is curt, but I don't know if I'm annoyed at Dad or the stupid little gnomes being silly.

Dad cocks an eyebrow and then smiles. "Oh, the ghost scones." He picks up an imaginary scone and pretends to eat away. "Hmmm. Better than, Mum's. Don't tell her that. She thinks she's a fine cook."

"No, Dad. Ghost gnomes, not scones. I found them. They're having a garden party. It's much more fun than yours. At least it was."

"A garden party with ghost gnome scones." Dad laughs.

"Not scones. They're real," I yell.

He rubs my hair, a little too roughly, messing it up. "Good. You coming, everyone?" Dad turns to the other adults and then wanders inside.

My heart sinks. I spent all this time waiting for them and he doesn't even care that they're real.

Stewie stumbles towards the esky like a dazed zombie. He smells like he's been barbequing grass in a pub. He glares down at me with red beady eyes, takes one step too many and kicks the esky. It jolts until it's dangling over the edge of the pool a few inches.

"Don't!" I lift the lid and see my gnomes frantically making for higher ground on the empty cans. I grab the esky handle. "Help me pull it back."

"You keep opening that thing, and my beer's gonna get warm. May as well be drinking piss."

I delve my free hand in the esky and hand him the

bottle of wine.

He snatches the bottle from my hands. "That's just dregs." He pours it on the tiles and throws it back in the ice water. He lifts out the empty can.

A tiny gnome clings to the ring-pull. It drags itself up and climbs inside the can.

Stewie shakes it by his ear. "Where'd all the beer go? Your parents haven't been teaching you early, have they?" Stewie asks me.

I ignore his question and reach up for the can. "Stop shaking it!"

"S'more inside." Mum's voice and legs are all wobbly as she walks past us.

"Mum, I need that can."

"Suuuure, cans." She keeps on walking and stumbles inside. It's lucky the door's open or she would've crashed right into it. "I'll get you cans," her voice trails off.

Stewie flips the esky lid shut again, almost jamming my fingers in there. Then tosses the beer can in the pool.

"No! He was inside."

Stewie saunters inside.

"Mum!" I call out but the racket inside drowns out my voice. I let go of the esky and it balances by itself. I race to the fence and grab one of the sticks Dad cut down. The bark grazes my hands as I drag it back to the pool.

I kneel by the esky and reach towards the can with the stick. I see my gnome looking out of the can opening.

"Hang on." I reach out further until my stick is inches from the can.

Shuffling my knees closer, I grab hold of the esky

with one hand and lean my whole body out. The stick reaches and the gnome jumps on, runs along the stick, wobbles, falls.

"No!" Without thinking, I reach out with my hand. My weight pulls me too far forward. I head dive into the pool. Cool water rushes over my skin and down the back of my clothing, and something hard hits the back of my head.

Night-time creeps across the water, dazzling light and then colour. A green wine bottle sails past my head, coloured cans, and the blue esky. Coloured gnomes swim alongside me and hold my hand. They are as large as I am now. Or am I as small as them?

"It's okay," they tell me.

I can hear them. And see them. They wear bright coloured clothing: fire-engine red, sunny yellow and gorgeous greens.

"You can enter our portal now and join us." They swim down and down, towards the pool grate. They wiggle through the slats. "Come on," I hear them call from the other side. I squeeze through the slats and out to the other side where a whole new garden party awaits.

Shifting

Hunched over, he ... it enters my office, approaching the couch with hobbled gait - fangs poised. Instantly, I regret agreeing to his request for a night-time appointment. Hidden behind the clouds, the moonlight casts a meagre ray of light into the room, which skitters across my desk and glistens upon his tangled fur.

On hind legs, he perches on the leather couch. "Doc! My head. Boiling fury. It'll return." His voice is ragged. Drool cascades onto the couch from the end of a razor sharp canine.

Wary, I stand behind my desk. But I've treated gargoyles and vampires and a pesky hobgoblin who wouldn't leave my office until I gave him a sock. So why should this appointment be any different?

"It wants to escape." Perched on all fours, he paws holes in my black leather sofa.

I pick up my notebook and pen, but keep the desk between myself and ... my client. "I'm not sure I can fix your shape-shifting," I say trying to steady my nerves. "I'm just a lowly therapist."

"The internal beast. You can tame it. It's crazy. Psychotic. It kills." His voice is guttural with angst. "Hundreds have died by the hands of the beast within."

Nerves get the better of me and I glance at the window, ready to take a leap, trying to judge whether I'd survive the fall.

Suddenly clouds part revealing the full moon.

"Arghh!" His haunting screech resonates throughout the room.

I drop my pen and notebook. "It's okay, just take a deep breathe." Take a deep breathe? What kind of advice is that? I must be losing my touch.

"Stop it!" he pleads. "You need to stop the beast within me." His head jerks backwards towards the moon.

"The...beast–" The popping of bones strangulates his words.

Keeping an eye on my patient, I fumble in my desk draw looking for my gun and silver bullets. My hand glances over wooden stakes for vampires and a shard of mirror for the cockatrice I've book for a "chat' next week. Finally, I find the pistol. I keep my fingers poised over the weapon. It's just a last resort. No matter how horrifying the monster, there is always a way to redeem them.

"...beast...will be," the creature tries to wrangle words into sentences, but his jowls curl and shrivel into fleshy pink lips. His skin twists like elastic, contorts and convulses.

"...it'll be...unleashed."

His limbs shrink and crackle into humanoid form. Wailing drowns out the bone crunching contortion.

And before me sits the man. "Run! I can't stop the beast..." He stands on the couch. "Run!"

From all that we flee

Aislin woke to see a tall blue alien guarding their cell. She sat bolt upright. Her hand automatically went to her head. Like a suffocating metal crown, the black device around her skull was still there. And her daughter was still gone.

Across the dusty pen, sat Hannaford. He hadn't spoken a word to her since they'd been imprisoned. He'd pretended he didn't know her, as if she were just another crew member. Their interlude on the ship may have been brief, but it meant something to her.

Aislin curled up on her side, hugging her knees. Stones dug into her ribs, but she didn't care.

Around her, the cage shone with walls of translucent insidious blue light. She wished they were opaque, then she could pretend she was somewhere else, maybe back on the ship with her beautiful little Kiesha. Instead, she was penned in with the rest of the crew like a dozen battery chooks and the unbearable smell of a week's" worth of fear and sweat.

"They took her." She looked up at Hannaford. She wanted him to reassure her, to hold her, the way he had on the ship. "They took our daughter. They took all of them."

He glanced at her. His rigid posture and pale skin made him look like an impenetrable slab of marble that no chisel could carve. He cast his eyes from her and tinkered with the dislodged halo perched on his lap. His indifference was like a million knives jabbing her heart. Who knew what they were doing to Kiesha, and he didn't care. He hadn't cried once. Not a single sob. Not a clenched fist. Nothing. It shouldn't have surprised her. He never wanted her. Kiesha was a mistake according to him. His words when he'd learned of her pregnancy still drilled into her subconscious.

"You can't bring up a child while we're still searching. What if we don't find a suitable planet?" Those words hadn't hurt her more than his final words on the matter. "You need to get rid of it.'

Not her. It. As if she was as insignificant as space junk that should be jettisoned into the black.

"Help us!" The logistics officer, Letitia, cried out from the other side of the pen, interrupting Aislin's thoughts. "Let us out." Letitia crawled across the hard dusty ground towards the blue wall of light, the same barbaric light that erupted from their weapons.

"Grab her!" Aislin said in a harsh whisper.

The technician, Jackson, and Hannaford grabbed her by the waist. "The light," said Jackson. "You can't.'

Letitia slumped to the ground just shy of the blue light.

"Your son," pleaded Aislin. "You need to stay for him." They'd taken all the other children, but Letitia's son looked so much older than his tender twelve years.

Thank heavens Kiesha was small. It was the one thing giving Aislin hope. Perhaps they'd taken them away to protect them and that it was only the adults they were torturing.

The only other youngster in the pens was a teenager. He didn't sob. He didn't speak. He didn't move. His father had tried to pry the halo off his teenage son. It took him and two other strong men each grabbing a side of the halo and levering it from his head. It was like watching a television blinking out during a power surge. There was light in his son's eyes and then pop—nothing. The halo sat on the dusty ground with long thin black tendrils running from it. Aislin had tried to distract herself by focusing on the halo, but eventually her eyes flickered sideways to the teenager. Just a glance. That was all it took, a glance and she'd seen the holes where those leach-like threads had drilled into his skull. His father had shaken him, hugged him, screamed at him until his voice cracked. He now just sat there with his teenage son's head resting in his lap. The father patted his son's hair as he sang the lullaby. The lullaby they all used to sing.

"We'll win the lottery. We'll fly away.
We'll find a new home. Where we can play.
I'll sing to you softly. I'll rock you to sleep.
Again we'll see sunshine. Now baby don't weep."

No matter how many times he sang it, the boy wasn't going to respond. But no one could convince him otherwise. He was a grieving father. He wasn't Hannaford. Hannaford hadn't shown any emotion when they'd snatched Kiesha as they clambered from the ship's wreckage. They'd made them watch as they forced the halos on all the children. On his little girl.

Beyond the blue prison, a door slid open on the silver cylindrical towers, and two aliens strode towards them. They approached: tall, slender, almost humanoid except for their sickly pale blue skin and heart-shaped heads with a similar halo around them.

There were no heavy footsteps, no batons banging against bars trying to intimidate their prisoners, just silent steps.

Hannaford crossed his legs and shoved the teenager's halo in his lap.

Those who had been taken for questioning spoke of the horrors. At least those who could speak. Letitia's son hadn't said anything, nor had a brother and sister who had worked in the shuttle. They just sat side by side. She nursed her elbow as if it were broken, but it looked fine.

The walls of blue light around them vanished as the aliens loomed over their heads. Many times, she'd thought of running when that happened. Running to find Kiesha. How far would she get before they stopped her?

"Small male will come." Even though they didn't move their tiny mouths, she heard the creature's voice in her head, as did everyone else, for all eyes looked around to see who they referred to. Two creatures wearing their own halos stood and pointed long blue fingers to the centre of our group.

Letitia screamed. "No!" She ran to her son just as the creature stepped through the crowd and tugged at the youngster's arm. "No. Please! Take me. He's just a boy."

The creature's halo twinkled blue and it waved a hand through the air. At the same instant, Letitia fell backwards onto the hard ground. She cradled her cheek with her hand.

"Learn, boy is pupae." When they spoke, blue lights danced upon the black metal of their own halos. "Will go to camps."

Aislin crawled towards Letitia. "It's okay," she whispered. "They think he's a child. They'll look after him, like they're looking after Kiesha."

"Is that what you think?" her voice was meek. She looked up at Aislin with wide eyes.

Yes, it had to be true. She hadn't seen a younger looking creature, but she had to believe they understood that children were innocent. Then again, they were innocent too and that didn't seem to matter.

The boy screamed as they dragged him from the others. Letitia got to her feet unsteadily at first and then with more resolve. "Give him back to me!"

"Don't," Aislin whispered, afraid her voice may attract attention.

"You can't take him." Letitia took a few tentative steps at first and then bolted towards the creature like a pistol. Her body rammed into the creature's legs. They tumbled in a tangled heap of blue and beige limbs. Aislin heard the creature groaning in her head. Despite the technology, they were still vulnerable. It gave her a miniscule ray of hope.

Letitia grabbed her son's hand and dragged him away as fast as she could.

While the aliens were distracted, they might've had the chance. If anyone was game enough. Aislin wasn't. She sat there, wanting to help, wanting to run to Letitia's aid, but she didn't move. No one moved as the other creature shot blue light, hitting both of them.

Gasps erupted from crew members behind her, but words and screams caught in Aislin's throat.

The son's skin began to blister first, then it peeled layer by layer. Shreds of skin fell away. The boy screamed, high pitched and painful to the ears. Letitia didn't; however her pain in her eyes was undeniable.

Aislin wanted to turn away, but she sat transfixed. The blue light of the pen re-emerged around them, but she could still see. For some unknown reason, she still watched.

The boy's skin was red now. Hands, face, bare

feet, every morsel of exposed skin melting away to the lower dermis.

Letitia clambered to her knees above her son. She mouthed something but no words emerged from her blistering lips. Then she placed her red peeling hands around her son's neck. Her jaw muscles poked through, her knucklebones protruded, but still she pressed down.

Aislin finally cast her eyes away. The son's screams died until all that could be heard was a father still singing a tender lullaby.

The sound of bodies dragging in the dirt cut through the father's song. She knew she shouldn't, but Aislin couldn't help but look. One alien dragged the dead son. The other clasped Letitia by her leg and lugged her away. Aislin swore that there was no way she could still be alive, but Letitia's exposed jaw muscles moved as if she were trying to speak.

Aislin's chest throbbed so much she thought she might have a heart attack. It would be an easy way out, to let herself die, maybe just stop eating the grey gloop they were fed every other day. She would do it, if it weren't for Kiesha.

"Ha!" Hannaford's voice cut through the despair and fear around her. The faintest hint of a smile flickered across his lips. What was wrong with him? Did he not care what had just happened? He cast a glance to the creatures as they strode back to their buildings. When they'd disappeared he took the halo from his lap. The outer casing had been cracked open. Circuitry buzzed beneath the surface: a blue and green pattern of lights. The tendrils vibrated and wrapped themselves around his thighs, but Hannaford didn't seem to notice.

"Jackson." Hannaford crept towards the technician and showed him the device.

Aislin crawled towards them as well. "Have you worked out how to get them off? How to get it off Kiesha?"

Doors slid open in the towering structures beyond the pen. Hannaford thrust the device into Jackson's hands, who placed the device behind his back.

"Have you worked out how to turn them off at least?" She felt left out, cast aside.

"Don't talk to me." Hannaford cast a glance that made her feel like a random atom in a galaxy.

"Hannaford! Please. Our daughter. She's out there somewhere. Hopefully alive. If you or Jackson have any way of stopping the halos. Please. I'll get out. I'll run as far as I can and find her before..." Aislin's voice trailed off. It was no use pleading with him. Hannaford wouldn't even return her gaze.

The blue light around them disappeared. She'd been so angry, so frustrated with Hannaford, that she hadn't even seen them approach. A blue spindly finger pointed in her direction.

She wasn't ready. She gazed at the soil, waiting for the inevitable and for the creature to drag her to her feet. To her doom.

"You understand me, don't you?" That was Hannaford's voice. "Because of your halos."

Aislin looked up to see Hannaford standing. "Don't. They'll shoot."

"I am the captain. Do you understand the word? The boss. Ask me questions," Hannaford commanded as if he were ordering his crew around.

Aislin shook her head. He didn't need to do that. He could show he cared, but he didn't need to sacrifice himself.

"She connected genetically?" The creature asked

and pointed to Aislin. "Both come."

"No. She is nothing to me." Hannaford stood, facing the creature. His tall frame looked tiny in comparison.

"She looks at you," the creature's voice filtered into her head. "Like the other genetically connected people look at each other."

"No. She means nothing," Hannaford said with a monotonous drone. "I promise she is not genetically related to me."

The creature grabbed Aislin's arm and pulled her to her feet.

"You don't need to take her." There was a hint of concern to Hannaford's voice, but he said nothing more as the creature led them from the group.

She was tempted to run, but would she get far enough to find Kiesha? Truth be told, she didn't know whether her legs would let her run. Gripped with fear they seemed to obey. Each dutiful step took them closer to the towers. The doors slid open. Hannaford entered in front of her, but she couldn't. She stood frozen until a cold breath wafted across the back of her neck. She looked up behind her to see a creature's blue head gazing down at her. It tapped her shoulder with its weapon. The tap dislodged a tear that she didn't know had been there. Had they taken Kiesha in here? Had they hurt her? Even if they hadn't, she must've been so scared. No, Aislin was scared. Kiesha must've been terrified.

"Can I see my daughter?" her voice was barely audible, but it didn't need to be for the alien to respond. It hit her on the back with its weapon making her stumble forward into the room.

Hannaford walked ahead. He didn't turn back when

she let out a gasping sob.

"Please!" Aislin didn't know if she were pleading to the aliens or to Hannaford to help her or at least show he cared.

The doors slid behind her. Based on the gleaming exterior, Aislin expected the interior to be sparkling silver, polished and neat, but the corridor leading to the interior was narrow and dark. Massive oval-shaped lamps cast dim blue light along the walls on either side of them. They crackled like flame without heat. She peered closer. Inside the light was a curled-up figure. They weren't lights, rather huge cocoons. A blue light shined bright inside each one. The crackling was the outer layers peeling off, like skin peeling off Letitia and her son from the blue weapons. The image of the mother and son's melting skin resurfaced and the acidic taste of bile filled her mouth. Up ahead, one of the cocoons split open and two large blue arms pushed the outer layers away. It emerged full-grown, as ghastly and terrifying as the rest of the aliens. She didn't have time to look much longer as she was ushered forward.

They walked down corridor after corridor. Turned left. Turned right. Left again. Aislin tried to recall the route they were led, but her mind was abuzz with images, and she felt at any moment she was going to heave.

At every step, they passed more and more cocoons dangling on the walls. Were these their children? Their pupae? If so, did they understand how scared their children would be? Did they understand that they couldn't treat them the same way they treated the adults? Maybe they'd taken them to see why they were smaller than the rest of the crew. Maybe they were experimenting ... Aislin's stomach couldn't bare it any longer. She heaved, regurgitating a grey mess onto the dark floor. The creatures showed no interest or sympathy they just pushed her through another door.

Thoughts had curdled in her brain so much Aislin had lost all sense of direction. They stood in a room so dark it felt as if all light had been sucked from it. The walls, the floor, the ceiling were all black. Too black. And frictionless. Aislin could barely feel the ground under her feet. Was this the room that the others had spoken about? The room where they'd all been questioned? The door slid shut and its outline vanished as if it had melted into the walls.

Claustrophobia set in. She began to hyperventilate. Air struggled to make its way past her throat. Blue lights started twinkling in the dark. From the lights of the alien's halo, she could just make out Hannaford standing there, perfectly calm. His presence should've reassured her. She desperately wanted to believe that he would protect her, defend her and that he'd make everything alright.

"Why you come?" The words that filtered into her head were surprisingly pleasant and quiet. Nothing like the guttural reprimanding tone she'd expected from the aliens.

Aislin gasped for breath.

"We've told you already," Hannaford responded, his voice, like his posture, was composed. "We just want somewhere to live. We won't disturb—" He suddenly gasped and keeled over.

"Hannaford!" Aislin found her breath and her vocal cords. "Stop it, you monsters!" She faced the aliens bracing herself for retaliation.

"Why she does not feel hurts too?" There was confusion in the alien's eyes.

"We're not related." Hannaford picked himself up off the floor, clutching his stomach.

The aliens voice sounded confused. "We not understand."

Hannaford screamed out. He clasped his arm.

Aislin ran towards him, but something hit her chest sending her stumbling backwards.

The pain in Aislin's chest tightened. Her ribs felt like they'd been hit by an anvil, her heart felt as if one of those creatures were plunging blue spindly fingers through her rib cage and squeezing.

"It's not real!" Hannaford yelled at Aislin. "It's just what they're imagining."

Aislin heard his voice but it barely registered. The physical damage might not be real but the pain – the pain was real.

"How you genetically related to the little human, but not each other?" the alien asked ignoring their pain.

"Little human." The words bypassed the pain. They meant Kiesha.

"What have you done to her?" She screamed, running without thought towards the blue twinkling lights. Before she reached it, her arm felt like it was on fire. She could feel her skin blistering, the rawness, the nerve damage. She hugged her arm to her chest. The creature was nowhere near her arm and yet it was so excruciatingly painful. She collapsed on the floor and rested her arm against the cool black surface. However, it didn't relieve the pain. The thought that Kiesha might have gone through any of this flickered into her mind again. Sweat beamed on her forehead, the pain in her chest escalated, and the burning, all her limbs were burning.

"Please, listen to me," Hannaford's voice echoed in

the background. "We told you why we came."

There was a pain to his voice, but he wasn't panicking. The pain in Aislin's limbs and chest slowly eased. They had relented. Hannaford's words had gotten through. Or so she thought. The questions started again. The same questions.

"Reveal to us, why you come?"

Aislin sat up and looked at Hannaford. Her pain had ceased so they must've been attacking him, but instead of screaming or writhing with pain he suddenly chuckled. He really had cracked.

"Notice anything?" Hannaford almost sounded cheerful.

The alien just looked at them.

"What are you trying to imagine now?'

The alien's eyes widened. Was that surprise?

"You're all identical. Don't think I haven't noticed. Perfect genetic clones," Hannaford said.

Aislin hadn't noticed, but thinking back she realised they were completely identical, even the ones that came out of the cocoons.

"Is that why you're so fascinated by our genetic connections, by our children? Your pupae hanging on the wall, they aren't from sexual reproduction are they? You don't understand relationships."

"It is waste of time." The creature's words filtered in Aislin's head. "Evolved beyond reproduction long ago. Time spent advancing. Creating cities." The alien looked around it as if he could see the city amid the four walls. "Our city. Our technology. Not for you."

"That's what I thought. You don't look at each other the way we do." Hannaford cast the slightest glance in Aislin's direction and there was something in his eyes she'd seen before. "You don't know what it feels like to not be able to hold someone you love. You don't know what it feels like to leave family on a planet that is doomed." Hannaford held her gaze.

A screeching noise filtered into her head. For a second she thought it was Hannaford, but he still stood there looking at her with adoration. She turned to see the alien doubled over clutching his stomach.

"You don't know what it's like to keep all your emotions bottled up to protect those you love. To feel it eating you up inside. Can you feel that?"

Aislin finally understood. Hannaford had been protecting her. And she had been letting all her emotions about her daughter flood out. It had been obvious from the start that she was pained by her daughter's capture. They must've known all along. Had she put her daughter at risk? The pain she'd felt in her chest returned, but it wasn't the alien's doing. The lights weren't twinkling on the alien's halo anymore.

"You speak, we all hear," Hannaford was still speaking and the alien was still bent over. It grasped its head and she heard a drawn-out mewing sound in her head.

"You imagine torture on one and those who are genetically related feel it. Your pain receptors can't be that different to ours, or your black halos wouldn't work on us. And Jackson has figured it out. It must've been pretty easy to reverse the feed." Hannaford looked impressed with himself, and Aislin had to admit she was in awe and smitten like the first time she saw him. "Except it's not just you feeling it, you're all feeling it. And what you're feeling I'm not imagining," he continued. "It's real. It's painful. And I'm betting your race hasn't felt that kind of emotional pain in a long *long* time. Unexplained pain that hurts everywhere."

The alien clasped its stomach, its chest and then its head again, as if it didn't know where the pain was coming from.

"Chest pain, burning and breaking bones? Really? That's the worst pain you can imagine?" He laughed, a dry hollow laugh that even made Aislin's hairs on her arm prickle. "Now, you want to feel real pain?" Hannaford walked right up to the alien and stared at him defiantly. "Where's my daughter!" Hannaford's voice echoed around the small room.

The alien opened its tiny mouth as if trying to speak, but it couldn't. It clasped its throat.

"Yeah, that one's a humdinger. That lump in your throat trying to suffocate you, that won't let you breathe. Real painful, hey? Do you have any idea what it's like to see something once cradled in your arms taken away from you, not knowing if you'll ever see her again?"

The alien extended a long finger and pointed at the door and then right. It looked up at Hannaford with wide eyes, clutching its throat.

"What? You want me to stop it. Well I can't. That pain isn't going to stop until I find our daughter." Hannaford walked over to Aislin and offered her a hand, helping her to stand. His eyes welled up with tears. There was every emotion possible in those eyes, anger, fear, rage, despair, pain and sorrow. And the creatures were all feeling it, feeling all of Hannaford's pain, and hers, Jackson's, the father's, all their pain.

They exited the door and turned right. Along the corridors dozens of lanky blue creatures were writhing in pain. As they ran hand in hand, Hannaford cast Aislin a look. Behind the pain, there was love and hope in his eyes, and she felt it too.

Hive mind

A school of Sand Scrapers are drilling towards the nursery, the surveyor caste calls to all of us.

They drive raptor-like claws and slender bodies through surface sands and cracked clay.

We see what the surveyors see. The sight fills our bodies with hatred, but not despair.

Sisters! Our leader's voice fills my mind. She needn't say more.

We must extricate them, the rest of my sisters agree in unison. My thoughts spill from my mind along with theirs. They are a threat. They must be eliminated.

This is simple. This is undeniable. This is what we do.

We stride through the underground tunnels and chambers: rucksacks perched upon our shoulders, spears steadied by our sides, daggers concealed in our leather belts. Our long-sleeved linen jumpsuits are light enough for fighting but covering enough to protect us from the vengeful sun. It shimmers low in the sky beyond the perpetual haze, but its fury hits us as we walk outside. In a single-filed convoy, we pile out of the antechamber, one by one.

Stay alert. Stay within contact of a fellow sister. The leader of our warrior caste relays her thoughts, but there is no need. We all know we cannot stray too far.

Survival depends on contact with one another. Survival of the colony depends on us.

Five injured, the surveyor caste relay to us. The saviour caste will be here soon, they inform us. We see them standing on the ridge with scanners and scopes. The surveyor caste sees five bodies strewn in the hot sand amid a pool of blood.

I see. I am reminded of the infants in the nursery. We can't let the Sand Scrapers get to them.

The image lingers longer than it should. It is not my job to worry about such things.

Targets are beyond the jagged outcrops, one of our sisters reveals to us.

I redirect my attention to the enemy.

Dozens of Sand Scrapers congeal on the blistering sands. Tails swish, flicking their body sideways and pushing the sand away. Pale scales shimmer in the dwindling sunlight like plates of gold.

We cannot see them with our own eyes yet, but we quicken our pace as the visual is relayed from sister to sister.

We follow our sisters" directions to a ridge of jagged ironstone rock. The Sand Scrapers are on the other side. The first of our sisters await us there so we can attack as one. We dart down the ridge, hopping from rock to rock.

We group together. The Sand Swimmers protective white scales reflect the sunlight with blinding intensified glare. Some have already buried themselves below the surface. Others" tails are still visible, swishing away.

Ready? we ask one another. Protect the nursery. Protect the colony, my sisters think.

We race across the sand. Heat radiates upwards. Sweat already beckons to drip from our temples. We hurl spears at the flicking tails. The Sand Scrapers stop their burrowing and turn in our direction. We draw daggers.

A second school of Sand Scrapers are charging from behind the outcrop, the surveyor caste call to us. They will be there in a matter of... the voices fail.

Have they fallen? No time to question. We must trust that the saviours will come to their aid.

The medley of visuals and words pound away in my head.

Behind us, one of our warrior caste falls as a tsunami of white scaled creatures descend upon us.

It is as if the Sand Scrapers lured us here. Have they learned to strategize?

Half of us turn to the onslaught approaching from behind. The other half attacks those still burrowing. To the left, a sister tumbles as a Sand Scraper's claws delve deep into her chest. The saviour caste will come. They will have seen the attack; their technology may be enough to save her. It is not for us to dwell on. And yet, I do.

A Sand Scraper is lurching behind me, a sister reveals. I raise my dagger, spin and drive it into the flesh between the Sand Scraper's tough scales. Blood trickles onto the red sands below as it slumps onto its belly.

The flurry of information ripples through all of us: Sand Scrapers burrowing to the nursery stop, they turn to us; those behind have grown in numbers, twenty, thirty, too many to count; another sister falls just over my left shoulder; the culprit approaches.

It raises its claws. A spear lies under its abdomen where our sister has fallen.

I dive roll under the creature, grab the spear, and thrust it upwards.

Blood sprays, soaking my hair. The injury infuriates the creature. It does not fall. Instead, its high-pitched wail echoes across the landscape.

A few Sand Scrapers fall as sisters thrust spears and slice daggers through scaled skin. The rest begin to flee.

I tug my spear, but the barbs jam under the scales. Yanking proves useless.

The creature bolts with me still attached. Others run too in a stampede of claws.

The spear becomes a lifeline. Let go and be trampled.

My sisters still slaughter the creatures that remain. I gaze through the stampede of clawed feet, my sisters dwindle in size as the Sand Scraper drags me further away.

Do they see?

Stray not far. That is our mantra. Stay in contact. Stay close. My clothes tear as abrasive sand rubs against my back and legs. I feel the first trickle of blood run down my spine, cool against my skin.

The Sand Scraper still squeals, drowning out my sisters" thoughts. It slows and stops on a sand dune. The other Sand Scrapers pelt past us and then begin to burrow, not to attack this time, rather to escape the heat and elements. They drill down until out of sight.

I still cling to the spear. My hands are blistered and raw. Do I let go? If so, where do I run? And where are my sisters?

I see nothing of the nursery grounds. I see nothing of the warriors or surveyors. No images. No voices echo through my mind. Have they all perished? Or have I strayed out of contact? I ... I, not we. Not us. Not our. Just me. There is no longer any "we'—just me. Alone.

Isolated. Separate.

I only see forward. I only hear the wind whispering in my ear, sand skittering over rock, a bird of prey squawking as it circles above. Has it come for the carcass, or does it know that alone in the heat my hours are numbered.

Defeated, my hands slip from the spear. It dangles under the Sand Scraper's belly like a massive splinter. The creature wanders forward and slumps in the hot sand, obviously too weary to dig like the others. The injured Sand Scraper looks as crestfallen as I feel. I roll onto my hands and knees and creep back the way it came, back towards my sisters.

Something rams my side. I hear my rib crack before I feel it. The sound accentuates the pain. I turn and catch a glimpse of The Sand Scraper's scaly body backing up as if to charge me again.

Where did it find that sudden burst of energy and how did I not see it coming? The answer sweeps through me instantly. I am alone. My sisters relay no information from behind me, alongside me, or from dunes beyond. I can see only forward. I can hear only around me. My chest tightens. My breathing hastens. I am truly alone.

The Sand Scraper lowers its bony head and rams me like I am as frail and flimsy as a fallen twig; nothing more than a toy to torment. The spear still in its belly rubs against the sand. More blood trickles from the wound. Is it too injured to kill me instantly? Is it trying to wear me down gradually?

It nudges me until I am on the precipice of a steep sand dune, almost vertical, falling away to sharp rocks below adorned with bones. It means to make me fall and spear me on the jagged stones. Clever. My sisters and I never gave them enough credit. The spear sways as the

Sand Scraper lumbers back, head bowed in attack posture. The Sand Scraper rams my chest again, winding me, knocking me off balance. I grab the spear. The Sand Scrapers eyes widen as it loses its balance too. It falls after me. My grasp on the spear slips. The Sand Scraper's heavier body slides down the sand faster, leaving a red trail of blood.

I try to dig my hands into the dune to slow my descent, but they slip through the soft grains as if it were air.

Sisters, I am falling. The voices have ceased. There is no way they can hear me.

As the rocks below loom near, the bones come into focus —a plethora of small reptiles and humans alike and the giant crustacean shells. I fling my legs beneath me and try digging them into the sand, but my weight just pushes the grains aside. Grit fills my mouth and hair. Below me, the Sand Scraper wails and swishes its tail, frantic to slow its descent. I get a gob full of fine sand. Wide eyes glance in my direction as it crashes headlong into the rocks. The wailing ceases.

I shift my weight to the left, in line with the Sand Scraper's body. My head crashes into its scaled body. It's harder than it looked, but not as hard as the rocks. The world blurs.

I can't pass out yet. I clamber over the rocks to the soft sands beyond and begin to dig. I keep scraping away sand. My hands are so raw they grow numb to the pain. My head spins, but I manage to drag myself into the ditch and cover myself with my rucksack before the sunlight completely vanishes and the night sucks all heat from the world; before the plethora of predators come out to play.

#

I awake to a dark sky and the sound of nearby crunching. As if splintered into a million pieces, my head aches and rattles with an unfamiliar barrenness. My ribs ache with each breath. A trickle of blood oozes from my temple and into my mouth: bitter but wet.

The crunching ceases. I want to peer out of my ditch; instead, I cower lower and shut my eyes. If my sisters were here I would see, but I feel blind and numb to everything around me.

A soft grunt echoes close. Too close. I tap my belt, feeling for my dagger. There is nothing sharp, just torn fabric, soft skin and sticky blood oozing from a gash. I open my eyes and peer beyond my rucksack. An elongated nose droops over the edge of my ditch and then a pair of fangs glint in the starlight. A gust brushes past, spilling sand onto my rucksack and filling my ditch with a smell as forsaken as moon-flowers. I pinch my nose while still trying to move as little as possible.

A claw delves into my ditch and taps my rucksack. It sniffs with its long nose then plunges its claws, ripping fabric from my sack. The creature chews on the fabric; spits it out; sniffs again. A claw delves at the side of my rucksack, narrowly missing my torso. It digs in the sand feeling around. It is only a matter of time before it prods me.

I ram my rucksack upwards stubbing its nose and scramble out of my ditch.

Vast expanses loom in all direction, barring the massive dune. I sprint towards it and try to run up the slope, but my feet slip through the sand and I tumble back down towards the Sand Scraper carcass. The flesh has been torn from the bone and ripped to shreds. It is scattered nearby, but barely touched. All that remains are ribcage, scull and a few scattered claws below that.

The giant fanged creature sniffs the ground, looks up with an eyeless face, nose drooping low. It hurtles towards me at astounding speed. It lunges. I duck at the last minute and pick up a Sand Scraper claw as it sails over my head. It lands in the soft dune, tumbles downwards. It is quick to its feet, but I am ready and drive the claw into its neck, slice it downwards.

Blood sprays as the creature falls. It drenches my once beige jumpsuit in its horrid stench.

Hairless and blind, the creature looks so innocent now, despite the size of those fangs.

At least I have food and weapons. I sheath the claw in my leather belt. It is torn, but there is enough Sand Scraper hide to fashion a new one, and enough meat to make a year's worth of jerky.

I collect the remaining claws and a few broken ribs. From the Sand Scraper's meat, I cut lengths of hide and strap the claws to what's left of my rucksack. Without my sisters, I can't see behind, but I can still defend myself if others attack my back. I shoulder my rucksack and start collecting the shredded meat. The creature splayed it out in a long line, perhaps it was trying to bury it for later. I follow the trail. My foot slips on the edge of a hole. Sand sprinkles down into the depths too dark to see in the dim light. The diameter is too small and round for a Sand Scraper's tunnel. If it's the fanged creatures burrow then it could be empty. It could provide sanctuary when the hateful sun rises. I know my time is limited.

I stick my ear to the opening. A whiff of that repulsive moon-flower smell wafts towards me, then yapping resonates from the depths. The noise intensifies. I shuffle back and reach for my claw, unsheathing it as four small white bare-skinned creatures emerge with drooping noses. Their pencil thin fangs snap away as they continue to call.

They surround me snapping at my knees, but somehow, I know they aren't trying to eat me. Their call is more a plead than anything else. Who knows why they flock to me? Maybe I smell as hideous as their mother did.

I don't know how I know this. There are no telepathic messages relayed. My mind is still blank to all but my own thoughts. Yet, I feel no fear like I did with their mother. Their mother that I killed. If all my sisters died, the infants in the nursery would not survive. Will these creatures?

I pick up a piece of Sand Scraper meat and toss it in their direction. In frenzy, they tear at the flesh, yapping at each other.

Heat burns the back of my neck. I turn to see the sun peeking above the horizon. The fanged beasts don't seem to notice. All their focus is on their food.

I drag a larger piece of meat to their burrow's entrance.

Come on, little ones. Follow the food.

I know they can't hear my thoughts but somehow they know what to do. Three from the pack grab the meat and tug it into their den, but the smallest remains sniffing at my legs.

Go on. "We can't stay out here." My voice startles me. It is hoarse but quiet, nothing like it sounds it my head. My words startle me even more. We. The word belongs to my sisters and me, not creatures that would rip us apart given half a chance. And yet, I don't feel guilt.

I grab another bit of meat and lead the smaller creature to the entrance.

"Come on." I sit at the edge of the hole.

It follows with its droopy nose sniffing the meat and my legs interchangeably. It nuzzles my leg, with fangs close, but doesn't try to bite or scratch.

I reach down and rub its forehead. It nudges my hand for another pat before grabbing the bit of meat in my other hand and disappearing down the hole.

"We'll be okay." I say it to reassure myself as much as them, because of course they don't understand me. So why do I say we? My sisters would never approve, but they don't need to know.

I slide in the top of the tunnel and watch the sun rise in the sky. How many other places like our world, bake under a blazing sun such as that? If there are others, can they cope alone or do they all need colonies like ours?

Questions. They erupt from nowhere and take hold. Before there were just voices, images, and constant stimulus, now my brain feels empty. All sorts of things are flooding in to fill the void.

Why are we bred to be warriors? What genetic traits does the nursery caste add to a surveyor, a saviour, a warrior, a nurse ... and a breeder? They say we all evolved parthenogenesis so why can't I have a family of my own. Why can I not be all these things?

Instinctively, I know the answer. Together we are strong. Separate we are weak. We have always been told that. And yet ... I managed to fend off a Sand Scraper. By myself. I am still here. Alone. Surviving.

Light fills the tunnel and with it comes the heat. The land swelters with the warmth of a billion candles. My jumpsuit sleeves are tattered and frayed. I use a claw to slice the sleeves off. A breeze darts down the hole and cools my sweaty arms, but even this far below the surface the sand is starting to bake.

On hands and knees, I crawl deeper until light and heat fail to reach me. Leaf litter scratches my palm and robust petals that feel like moon-flowers. The stench barely registers anymore but it still inflames my nostrils. Every logical bone in my body tells me to climb back up and endure the heat, not down, and yet my instincts drive me further into the depths. The leaf litter ceases and the sand under my hands and knees is damp. The tunnel opens up into a cavernous space. A few grunts welcome me and a cool nose rubs against my palm.

It is nothing like the structured antechambers and tunnels of my sisters', but it feels safe.

I place my rucksack, claw side up, in the tunnel and hope it is enough to deter intruders.

The grunting subsides and a subtle snoring takes over. I curl up against my fanged babies and sleep for the first time in ages without the voices in my head waking me every few minutes.

#

A Sand Scraper is clawing at our tunnel. It drills down my hole, sniffs, then thinks better of it. Instead, it devours leftovers from its fellow comrade on the dune in cannibalistic barbarism that makes my stomach curdle.

My baby fanged creatures sense the intruder and rouse from their daytime slumber.

"It's okay," I whisper to them. "It doesn't like the smell."

The tunnel is pitch-black and yet I know all this ...

and more.

A pack of Sand Scrapers gallivant in the plains to the west.

The nursery ground is safe again. The dead bodies strewn above the nursery are beginning to smell.

Below the dune, the coast is clear and the unforgiving sun has slept at last.

My babies are not satisfied the threat has gone. They tread further into their chamber and vanish down a side tunnel.

"Wait!" They do not listen.

Sister! I hear their calls as they search for survivors.

The voices and images return. They intensify. They stand at the top of the steep dune. My sisters. But they are different. Their jumpsuits are complete; their hair is neatly braided; their weapons are sleek and newly crafted. They don't carry the blood of friend and foe.

For some reason I crawl further down the tunnel. Everything goes blank again, and I am left alone in the dark, seeing nothing, hearing nothing, but smelling a faint trail of moon-flowers. I follow the scent. I can't let them come in range again. If they sense my thoughts, they will continue to search for me, to save me. But a tiny voice—my own voice—tells me that I don't need to be saved.

Silence Broken

Louis stumbled out of the portal, landing hard on his knees. Behind him, the iridescent blue portal of light swirled like an oceanic vortex. He shielded his eyes from the glare as the portal spun from a startling large conical mass to a pinprick and then popped out of existence.

This was it; this was the place. He recognised the hill and the lighthouse immediately. The sun glistened on its windows with a lime-white glare and the grass smelt freshly mown. This was the right place, but was it the right time? He gritted his teeth; a lump cloyed in the back of his throat as he struggled to his feet. Pulling back the cuff of his suit, he set the alarm on his watch: twenty minutes until the Time Corporation returned him to his own time and his own reality – one hundred thousand dollars for twenty minutes of hope. He leant on his wooden cane and peered up the hill. At five thousand dollars a minute, his old knees would've appreciated the Time Corporation opening the portal further up the hill.

On their first camping trip here, Marie and Louis had sprinted up the hill and fallen on the grassy slopes together laughing.

"We should come here every year," Marie had said as she lay on the grass.

Louis had sat watching her; her cascading hair draped through the unmown grass.

"Are you listening to me, Louis?" Marie had prodded him in the ribs.

He smiled. "Sorry, did you say something?"

"Stop messin" about. You heard me."

"Yes, we should come here each year. We can make it our place." Louis touched her cheek. "We can bring our children here."

"Children!"

He'd never forgotten the look of surprise on her face and how it had transformed into a smile.

"Let's not get too carried away. How about we start with something simple – like a puppy."

Louis had plucked strands of grass, taking deep breaths. "You know if we are getting a dog together we should probably make things...official."

Louis's chest tightened. Whether it was the trek up the hill or the memory, he wasn't sure. So much had changed since then. He certainly couldn't bend down on one knee now and he longed to feel that happy again. Decade after decade had passed and then the Time Corporation had made their services commercial. Finally, there was hope. He took a second job, sold their home and took out a loan. But it would all be worth it. He couldn't put a price on this visit and the chance of seeing her again.

As he reached the top of the hill he bent his knees; they grated and creaked like an old rocking chair. He had changed, but this place was exactly as he recalled. The air still had the same salty freshness and the ocean still sang with the same gusto. Below, the waves crashed upon the rocks and the water sang as it was sucked back into the blue abyss. The ocean spanned to the end of the world and merged into the sky in a three dimensional blue canvas.

He looked around; she wasn't here. Perhaps he was too late. Cautiously, he peered over the edge of the cliff. Sea lions grunted with content and seagulls cawed: tiny white specks darting above the jagged rocks. Louis stepped back relieved. He looked at his watch - ten minutes to go. Where was she?

He ambled to the lighthouse and sat on the doorstep. The smell of fresh paint overcame the smell of salt in the air. The seagulls" squawks diminished as the sun lost interest in the world and began to sink into the sea and then out of nowhere, gasping sobs overcame the cries of the gulls. She rushed up the hill; her hair shone as bright as the light above. Louis's stomach churned as if seagulls were pecking at his innards: a mix of nervous guilt and a hint of longing. He had almost forgotten her face. So focused on her, he almost forgot why he was here. Her feet were poised inches from the edge. He leapt up with agility contradictory to his age. "Wait!"

She spun to face him, her nose and eyes red. "I'm sorry... I didn't realise... I didn't see you." She wiped her nose on the sleeve of her knitted sweater.

"Are you okay?" Why did he bother asking that? He knew exactly how much pain he had caused her.

Through sobs and sniffles, she spoke in that angelic voice he so loved. "Yeah, I'm fine." She managed a wry smile.

"You don't look okay."

"I am. I'm fine." Marie clutched her stomach, her baggy sleeves dangled over her hands – the one Marie's mother had knitted at least two sizes too big.

"Fine...is that supposed to be an acronym? Frankly, I'm neurotic and emotional?"

Through rivulets of tears, she chuckled.

"What's so amusing?"

She shook her head. "It's just my husband says

that all the time."

"Really?" He glanced away; scared she'd see through his wrinkles.

"Although..." she added smiling. " He tends to replace "frankly" with something less refined. You could teach him some manners. He might listen to an elder. He never listens to anything I say."

"I'm sure that's not true."

She huffed and looked down at the ocean. "You don't know what he's like."

"Are you both camping here?" he asked hurriedly, trying to draw her attention upwards.

"Yes. It's our one year anniversary." Marie turned to the lighthouse. "He... proposed to me here."

"That must be a very special memory," said Louis. "You should keep this place special, where nothing bad should ever happen." Louis looked down at his watch. He was losing time. "I'm sure he's wondering where you are."

"Not likely. He's in one of his *moods*." Marie clasped the back of her neck with both hands and looked up at the sky, tinted in bands of turquoise and amber. "Sorry. I shouldn't be boring you with my problems."

"Please continue. If you bottle things up you…" He couldn't finish the sentence. He took a deep breath before continuing. "Silence isn't healthy."

"I can't talk about it."

Louis was losing ground. He had a speech planned out, but words were failing him. He could just grab her, grab her and hold her. He didn't need to return; he could stay here.

Louis's thoughts cascaded together in a blur. If he failed this could be the last time he would see her face. He looked at her pale hand and longed to hold it, to feel her skin. His fingers extended towards her, they were mere centimetres apart -

"He said he hated me," she said and tears started trickling down her cheeks.

Her sudden outpouring of emotion started him. "What? I..."

Marie raised an eyebrow.

"I mean, I'm sure he didn't mean it. Beautiful young girl like yourself... He couldn't have meant it."

She looked back across the ocean. "No, he never does."

His mouth felt dry; his tongue stuck to the roof of his mouth as he tried to speak, but there were no words. No words could possibly undo the pain he had caused her. The sad thing was he couldn't even remember what had started the argument – something as silly as money. He couldn't lose her again. "Please, I beg you. Just talk about your problems with your husband. Just come back away from the edge."

She looked down at her feet. "What...oh, I would never... I'm fine. Really."

Louis peered over the edge of the cliff. "Still, it would make me feel better if you moved closer to me."

She took a step backwards. "I'm fine. I just needed some fresh air. I just needed to remember the better times." The wind wafted up the cliff and she folded her arms over her torso.

"Promise me that you won't do anything rash. I need to know you will be okay before I go."

"I swear on Rocky's life." She laughed to herself. "Sorry, internal joke. I promise."

Rocky – he had forgotten how much she loved that crazy mutt. A pang of guilt shot to his stomach. She would never have forgiven him if she knew of Rocky's fate. But of all the promises she could have made, that was the one he could believe. She would do anything for that dog. He knew she was going to be okay and if she was okay then he would never have abandoned Rocky. If she was okay then everything would be okay.

His watched beeped.

She looked at him intently. "Do you have somewhere you need to be?"

"Yes. I have to go." Louis peered down the hill. "And when I wake the birds will sing not caw and my beautiful wife will be in my arms."

He had said too much. All of a sudden, he felt exposed. "Well Marie, it was nice seeing you," he said, avoiding her gaze.

"Yes, it was nice to meet you too. Thanks for listening."

He walked down the hill with a bound in his step. He knew Marie and that sparkle in her eyes. She wasn't going to jump. At the bottom of the hill, the dazzling light of the portal opened. He took off his watch and threw it on the slopes. Time meant nothing anymore; he would wake up with a lifetime of new memories with her.

#

Marie gazed across the ocean, the silver tips of the waves glistened in the light of dusk. A slight sea breeze wafted on her face. She loved this place. Its silence and tranquillity was calming: no tourists chattering or traffic honking. Even the seagulls had given up squawking and retired for the night. This place brought back happy memories. She cradled her stomach again. So many happy times. "Your daddy and I will make things work. He really does love me. He will love you too," she spoke softly to her stomach.

That crazy old man had no idea what he was saying. There was something odd about him though. She didn't even recall his name... she did not even remember introducing herself... She turned. He was but a silhouette at the bottom of the hill.

A circle of light suddenly perforated the sky on the horizon. She squinted and saw the man leap into a startling blue vortex. Then a blinding flash pierced her retinas. She held up her arms shielding her eyes from the glare and staggered backwards. Her foot found nothing but air. The cliff crumbled.

On the jagged rocks below, the seagulls awoke, breaking the silence and cawing in the night.

Shadow harvest

Sorath's sunlight blazed through the open door, as the stranger strode inside Sheriva's pub. Its glare illuminated dust particles hanging in the air before they combusted like minute firecrackers.

The bustle of chatting and glasses clinking ceased. The newcomer entered leaving the door ajar. He wore a typical hoodie and sunglasses, but strutted to the bar with a swagger unfamiliar to Sheriva's little abode.

"Shut the door!" She pointed a knobbly finger at the stranger. "Do you live in a bloody furnace?"

The stranger shrugged and flicked the door shut with his foot.

Sheriva patted the whip resting by her hip making sure she hadn't left it in the cellar. Nothing looked right about this character. She swirled the dregs of gin around in the bottle, tapped the counter twice and gazed upon her new patron. "Am I pouring?" she asked with as much graciousness as she could muster.

He pulled back his hood as he approached the bar. "How much for a whole bottle?"

"Good couple of inches." Sheriva pulled a candle from under the bar and lit it with a match; the orange glow illuminated the dim scenery around her.

The man pulled his hand away from the flame. "I want ice too." He perched his shades upon his shiny bald head. "Never understood why people keep their shades on inside." He nodded towards Sheriva's own goggles.

"Because idiots like you don't know how to shut doors and seem intent on frying us all." Sheriva scowled underneath her own hood and tinted goggles. "Ice is extra."

"I realise that." The man held up a finger in front of the flame. The candle cast a shadow equal to the man's finger, and it kept growing down the bar like a king python. "Enough?" he asked.

She nodded. "I'll take it all now." There was something in his eyes she didn't trust. The smooth skin, barely tarnished by Sorath's fiery glare, was unnatural.

"I have a blade," she began.

"No need." He drew his own, a small flick knife. It's blue hue shone as he sliced his shadow.

Sheriva pulled a vial from her robes, tilted it towards the shadow, dipping the lip into the darkness, and let his detached shadow slink into her stash. "You've had *good* times?" she asked attempting to subdue her interest.

He smiled. "Are you keeping that for later?" He nodded towards her vial.

"I don't need it yet." She placed it in the deep pockets of her robes. "This place is well protected." She poured the gin and left space for the promised ice.

"Yes, I saw the forest's shadows outside buffering this place."

I bet you did. Sheriva scooped a generous handful of ice from the cooler box, savouring the coolness against her skin.

"Seems a waste," he continued, "leaving the shadows to protect a forest of random trees. Those shadows must be worth a fortune."

She plonked the ice in his drink, letting the alcohol splash on the counter.

Wherever he got his shadows from wasn't through manual labour. His lily-white hands probably hadn't seen a days" work in their lives. That unscorched skin didn't belong; not a single scale, burn or crust flaked from his bones. He may as well have been made from thistle sap.

"Nice bar though." He swirled the gin around in his glass letting the ice cubes clink as potently as coins rattling in a purse.

Several of her regulars turned.

Did this bloke have a death wish?

Her regular, Mack approached with his lantern. The dim tea-light shone upon his well-worn, pockmarked face. That was the face of someone who'd been outside in the sun and slums. He placed his hand in front of the light casting a stub of a shadow.

"Mack." Sheriva raised an eyebrow. "You can't afford it. I won't take any more from you. You'll fry like a de-shadowed tree. I don't need my best customers ending up as Sorath's next sacrifice."

"I have a days" work lined up harvesting shadows from the northern forests," said Mack.

"And how do you intend to get there, without your own shadow?" asked Sheriva.

Mack shuffled on his feet unsteadily. "I'll pay you when I return."

"I don't run a bleeding charity."

Mack peered to the stranger. "Care to help out a fellow lover of gin." He smiled a lopsided grin.

"Not particularly." The stranger made an exaggerated effort to pull his glass closer to himself.

Sheriva noticed Mack tap his blade with a nervous twitch.

"Hardly seems fair keeping all that shadow to yourself," said Mack. Sweat beaded at his temples and around the rim of his sunglasses.

Don't do it. Sheriva glared at him.

Mack pulled his blade. Sweat ran past his sunglasses zigzagging around his face etched with Sorath's glaring wrath. "Did you slash all your shadows from kids in the underground slums?"

Sheriva was thinking the same thing. How many desperate kids and workers had he stripped of their only protection? "I hope they didn't come from any orphaned children. I'm very protective of them," said Sheriva.

"I guarantee that's not the case." The stranger smirked. "Bulldust! However you got that much shadow, you don't deserve it!" Mack thrust his blade in the stranger's direction, but missed. His blade sliced against the bottle of gin knocking it onto the floor.

Sheriva leaned over the bar, grabbing Mack's arm before he could strike. She twisted his forearm until he squealed and dropped the knife.

Mack fell to his knees, mouth agape, clutching his arm.

"Thank you," said the stranger, examining what remained of his bottle.

"That wasn't for your benefit." She hopped up onto the bar, swung her legs over to the other side, and helped pick Mack up to his feet.

"Still, I appreciate it."

"Two rules. You would've seen the sign," she said to the stranger. "No bar fights. No taking shadows from my forest trees." She turned her attention to Mack. "Sober up. If you're lucky I'll let you do some dishes to earn enough shadows to get you through a couple more days."

He stumbled away to the far corner of the pub, and slumped into a chair in shock.

"I'll get you a new bottle from the cellar." Sheriva brushed broken glass into her hand and disposed of it under the counter.

"Why's your extra booze in the basement?" asked the man. "Isn't this a bar?"

"Bar brawl last month. A woman smashed a man's head open with a bottle." Sheriva walked away from him to the end of the bar and down a short flight of stairs. She removed the key from around her neck and entered the cold room. Bottles of booze stood next to two dozen kegs. She manoeuvred around a large barrel that cluttered the floor and collected a fresh bottle of gin.

"Here," she said as she locked up and returned to the bar.

The man attempted to unscrew the lid. His white knuckles turned even whiter as he twisted and failed.

"They aren't working hands," Sheriva noted. She used the hem of her cloak to unscrew the lid. "Mack had a legit question. Where'd you get the shadows?"

The man poured a generous amount of gin into his glass, taking extra care not to spill any. "I run a consortium looking for new forests for shadow harvesting. Our company would provide reasonable compensation for your tree's shadows."

"No."

"When I say "reasonable', I mean enough to buy a pub a thousand times more glamorous than this one." He sipped his drink with a smug look.

Sheriva glanced around at the dim room and its patrons. The carpet was a bit sticky these days, the curtains were frayed, but it was home.

"Every tree sacrificed to Sorath just empowers him. The more Sorath acquires the more shadows we need to take. So the answer is still no."

"We are asking nicely now, but if the answer remains no, we will compulsorily acquire your shadows and your trees will burn." The man sloshed down the rest of his drink in two gulps. He sucked an ice cube before crushing it in his teeth.

Sheriva screwed the lid on the gin bottle tight. "No."

"Burn it'll be then."

"No it won't," she replied politely. Sheriva pushed the bottle of gin towards the man. "I think it's time for you to leave."

He chuckled. "I'll go, but you will also leave when your business goes under." He pulled up his hood, he looked at his sunglasses and then tossed them aside. "When you have as much shadow as I do, they're really just a fashion statement." He strode out the door, leaving it hanging open. Several of her patrons darted out of the way, as Sorath's heat blazed inside.

She scooted over the counter and followed him slamming and locking the door behind her.

"Mister!" she addressed him with disdain. "You forgot this." She thrust the bottle of gin in his direction.

"Keep it. You'll need all the assets you can get once we take your shadows. Unless you want to visit the underground slums and spend your life in regret and darkness."

Sheriva flung the bottle at his feet. Glass smashed against the hard dark earth. From her cloak's deep pockets, she pulled out her lighter.

He laughed. His shadow extended with each hollow cackle until it grew as tall as her trees. "Do you think you're going to burn off my shadow with flame and a bit of booze?"

Arrogant prick. She took a few paces towards him, leaving the shade of her pub. Sorath's heat blazed upon her exposed cheeks. She savoured the pain. Sheriva pulled out her whip and ignited the end with her lighter. She lashed her flaming whip against the smashed bottle. Blue light ignited and spread across the ground in a large radius engulfing his feet. His shadow detached and slunk back towards her pub.

Still holding onto his smug smile, the stranger clapped slowly. "That was just a waste of good booze." He rolled his eyes as his shadow regrew.

"Children!" She glanced up into her forest's canopy to see half a dozen children appear high up in the branches. Dirty faces of orphans, who had seen too many days in the slums, peered down at her. "Now!"

One of the children threw a bottle at the man. Sheriva lashed her whip into the liquid. Blue light travelled up his legs, severing the newly formed shadow.

A new shadow formed, and he pulled his knife, shining with blue vengeance. "Are we really going to play this game? It could go on a while."

"Maybe." She glanced up at a young girl in a tree a few feet behind him and gave her a nod. A bottle smashed by his feet and Sheriva smacked her whip down again. His shadow fled towards her pub with the rest.

He lunged with his knife, but as he did so a keg fell from the canopy to the ground. He stumbled over it.

Sheriva whipped the liquid spilling from the keg and watched the blue engulf his body. His shadows slunk across the dirt like flashes of dark.

The stranger's eyes widened and the smirk plastered across his face faded. He pushed past her to the pub and tugged on the door.

The tang of burnt dust lingered in the air. She inhaled deeply as blue light surrounded her feet and ran up her legs and torso. "Something wrong?"

"Where—?" He tugged on the door again before turning back to her. "Why aren't your shadows detaching?"

She pulled back the hood of her cloak and ran a hand over her scaly scarred head feeling the lumps and rough skin.

Disgust filled his eyes.

She drew back her goggles. "Because I don't have any shadows."

His disgust turned to shock. "You have all these shadows here and you let that happen to you?"

"It startles you? The redness, the scarring? Mister Lily-white, time to toughen up."

He stood in the narrow strip of shadow alongside her pub. "Let me inside," he pleaded. "I have powerful allies. They'll hunt you down if you don't."

She shrugged. "This place is protected by the two most vulnerable things in the world." Sheriva turned her back on him and strode to the backyard of her pub. She opened a trapdoor and climbed down the ladder into her cool cellar. "Two kegs ought to do it." She hauled them up the ladder, one by one. "Children!" she yelled over distant cries. She tried to block out the stranger's screaming as Sorath scorched his shadowless body.

Her children gathered around with their burnt and tarnished skin. "Here." She unscrewed the lids on both and inspected the darkness inside. "Empty half on my trees, and take the rest back with you to the slums." She pulled her hood back over her head and reaffixed her goggles in place. "I'll have more tomorrow, around happy hour again."

Something heavy dragged her cloak down. She reached into her pockets and found her vial. "Here," she said, handing it to the smallest girl.

The girl smiled with chapped lips and grimy cheeks. With a whole vial to herself, she still tipped half on a tree first before running off back to the slums.

Sheriva smiled. Returning to the front door, she kicked a pile of black ash out of her way before walking into a sea of silent faces. "Why so glum?" she asked turning to Mack and her other patrons. "Did I forget to mention, it's happy hour?"

###

The Red Goddess

My Red Goddess first died in front of me when I was six. The tiny wooden men with red heads brought her to me. She sat on the dry lawn and cackled a hearty laugh that set my heart ablaze.

"What's your name?" she asked.

"Mack," my voice quivered with excitement.

"I'm Kardla." Her cheeks flushed as rosy as the sunset. Her hair flickered like wisps of candle light in the breeze. And before I could tell Kardla how much I adored her, Dad approached waving a hessian sack in his hands.

"Get inside!" yelled Dad.

"I'll return," she whispered to me.

Return? Where are you going?

"They fear me." She crackled upon the grass. "And they should."

I don't.

"I know..." her voice trailed off as Dad held the sack over her amber head, choking her.

"Dad, what did you do?"

He grabbed the scruff of my t-shirt and dragged me away from the sooty black mark that was once my beautiful goddess.

"Mack, are you insane!" he yelled.

I guessed love was a kind of insanity, but Dad never understood.

#

At university, I met her again. I spent a glorious night watching my goddess dance on twigs and logs piled high. Drunken teenagers surrounded her naked body. She twisted and turned in ways no man could imagine possible. Jealousy grew in me, but as other students passed out, I sat and waited for our chance to be alone. As the night deepened, she faced me. Me alone. Wild eyes, wild hair and lips that would put Snow White to shame turned in my direction.

"Hello again, Mack," she spluttered, inebriated from too much alcohol forced down her tender throat.

I approached with the naivety of a boy never touched and rested my hand upon her heart. Her warmth radiated through me, but it did not hurt.

I missed you, Kardla.

"I know," she whispered and held me tighter.

We danced as if we were the only two on this earth until I could stand no more.

When I woke, some stupid boy with stupid glasses was drowning her with buckets of water. Her head lay in the ashy mud, the light fading from her glorious eyes. She glanced at me.

"They fear me," she hissed with her last breath.

I turned on the murderous four-eyed boy and smashed his glasses into his face. I defended her and the university expelled *me*. Like Dad, they didn't understand.

#

"Run!" Older and wiser now, I know everyone hates her. She must flee.

The orange halo surrounding her supple body deepens to a divine scarlet. "I'll crush them this time. We will be the last two standing on earth." Her raspy tones echo deep within my chest until I can feel my ribs shudder with every heartbeat.

"There are too many." My hands grip the steering wheel until my knuckles throb. "I can't see you die again."

Pain fills her amber eyes. "For you."

She brushes her fingers through rank fields of wheat. A gusty hot wind excites her, gives her life, and then she is sprinting, flying up the hill.

I follow in my car up an old dirt track towards an ironstone ridge. I would follow her to the end of the earth. I would drink the entire ocean so she could leave this land if she wanted.

Her voice crackles as she wraps her arms around a gum tree and climbs high. The eucalyptus scent clears my head and fills my heart. I climb the tree and embrace her warm touch. For a moment, I am lost in a haze.

Wailing interrupts us: a monotonous high-pitched squeal that saturates my ears.

I drop from the tree and brace myself as a truck approaches. Its red flashing lights blink menacingly. I glance up. She leaps with a ballerina's grace from tree to tree, trying to flee the truck.

A stocky man disembarks and strides towards me. He barks orders to other men inside the vehicle.

He is a devil in yellow overalls. His hard hat obscures his horns, but it cannot conceal the loathing in his eyes. He wants her dead. The other men that pour out the vehicle, dragging hoses and knapsacks, want to drown her.

"I guess our time is up again," she whispers.

"Mate, get out of here! It's not safe," the chief yells over her beautiful voice.

"Defend yourself," I plead with her. "They want to hurt you."

"What the heck are you yapping about?" asks the chief.

The other men shoot her with their fire-hoses. The water knocks her from the tree branch. She lies on the ground; her eyes bloodshot; her ruddy complexion begins to fade. Her agile flight is reduced to a sombre limp as she struggles across the ironstone towards the truck.

Kill them first!

For a moment, it looks as if she hears my warning. She rubs her back against the truck leaving a sooty trail of hatred, before turning on me. Her approach dazzles me. My face flushes with lust and longing. She knows the end is near, and in her dire time of strife, she wants to be with me. Only me.

Before she approaches to say goodbye, someone drags me away and takes me to the local town hall where everyone has fled out of fear of my beautiful goddess.

I wander down the street, and light a cigarette to console me.

On the edge of town, the old football oval is dry and lifeless. I flick the cigarette onto the grass and see her ignites again giving the world life.

"Mack." She spreads her arms wide, touching every blade of grass, inviting me to her.

I approach and relish in her sizzling embrace. Her touch is warm, but she will never harm me.

She climbs twigs and leaves, fence posts and trees. They think they have won, but like a phoenix, I will make sure she keeps rising from the ashes.

###

Look inside

"Look inside!" insist the blue and orange letters above the e-book's graphic design monstrosity. I click two stars and hit the back arrow to review another book. Static flashes. Misaligned paragraphs dance across the page as the preview opens.

#

You watch his pallid sallow skin glisten in the sunlight like a 22-carat diamond studded ring under disco lights.

"Hello," he says. As he talks his chiselled jaw slices through the air like an axe cutting wood; his razor-sharp canines gleam like popsicles defrosting in the morning sun.

You tremble.

#

Two stars was too kind. I hit the escape button, but I'm still staring at the e-book's preview.

#

He is so beautiful you wish you could shrink him and place him in a snow dome as a souvenir.

"I've seen you before," he whispers ever so softly.

#

Something white and papery falls on my keyboard, like snow from a snow dome. Nonsense. I hit the back arrow. The preview remains.

#

He ~~lies~~ ~~lays~~ puts you on a mattress. You feel like you've known him for at least a week, but he's undoubtedly and indisputably the love of your life.

He kisses your toes. You really hope he doesn't find that verruca you've been trying to remove for the last month. But it feels awesomely good. He plunges his razor-sharp vampire teeth into your leg like a razor-sharp drill drilling wood.

"OUCH!!!" you scream loudly.

He smiles hauntingly and sinisterly.

He sits next to you and pulls off a black t-shirt with five yellow stars on the front.

"You know you want to." His eyes mesmerize. Stars. Five yellow stars shining at you from his soul.

#

Blood trickles down my leg. "What!?" I hit control, alt, delete. The spinning blue halo of death tries to freeze my laptop, but the preview is still there.

#

Your hands are looking very pale, as pale as an anaemic polar bear. A doctor might say you have low iron, but if you look in the mirror, you'd see red-stained eyes and then you wouldn't see them at all because you wouldn't see your reflection because you would no longer be you (because you would be a vampire).

Instead, you'd just see the plush soft scarlet red velvet sofa behind you.

#

My soft isn't red; it's burgundy. So the book can't be talking about me.

#

The sparkly man is approaching your door, walking along the path, carrying an axe, wearing his t-shirt, which has five stars, which are all yellow.

By the way, burgundy is a type of red.

#

I peer out the front door and see no one. I return to my laptop. The book preview's finally gone and I'm left looking at 2416 customer reviews with an average of five stars. I hit the fifth star and get out of there. But I can't escape. Every internet site keeps telling me there is a new best seller today.

Elementability

Meeka's first words should have filled me with awe, but when my gorgeous little girl pronounced "argentum" there was just one emotion: fear.

It was a gurgled sound, but the word was unmistakable, and if we did have doubts, the blade of grass in the bio-dome turning to silver confirmed our suspicions.

"Sherie, she can't stay here," whispered Mack. He started packing away plates and cups and wrapping the loaf of stale bread back in the cloth. "Come on, get off the picnic rug."

It was all happening so quickly. One minute we had a normal beautiful baby girl, the next... What was I thinking? She was still beautiful. She was just... special. She was still the most special baby ever.

"They aren't taking her." I sat on the picnic rug in an act of defiance, and let Meeka clasp my index finger with her tiny hand.

She smiled, blowing a raspberry as she did so.

Mack squatted down and untangled her tiny fingers from me. "You don't know what she might do."

"She won't hurt us."

"What like she didn't hurt that blade of grass?" Mack's voice elevated.

The family picnicking under the withered Monument Tree turned in our direction. Their two boisterous sons ran in circles around the tree. While the boys didn't notice the tension unfolding here, their parents did. The mother smiled and gave a little nod as if she understood the difficulty dealing with family, but I doubted anyone could understand the mix of emotions welling inside me.

There was no way the family could see the blade from that far away, but nonetheless Mack stood in front of the silver, trying to conceal the evidence. To them Meeka must have appeared to be another normal baby. Normal? With the denuded alien landscape outside, the word held little meaning.

"We have to go, now," said Mack.

"Where?"

"Back to the camps, maybe? I don't know. But someone is going to notice."

"It took us so long to work our way here. The camps are no place for Meeka."

"Let's just go back to our quarters and figure out our next move." Mack stacked everything in our basket.

I nodded, but a lump cloyed in my throat. How could this have happened? We hadn't spent that much time near the Seam. Or maybe we had. We picked berries there during my first trimester. Was that enough? Was this my fault? Food had been scarce that winter. It was either forage or beg for scraps at the camps.

"Gaga," Meeka cooed.

Mack and I both looked around. We looked for changes, but nothing had materialised, nothing had transformed, at least nothing we could see. She could have created some toxic gas. No one would ever know. How would we know if she did that at home? It was my first hint of doubt. How could I question whether or not we could look after her? We had to; she was our baby.

Mack must have seen the confusion in my eyes as he squeezed my hand. "I think it was just normal baby talk," said Mack. "I'm not suggesting anything, but the Elemental homes are an option. We have options."

No. I had intended to say the word aloud and confidently, but my inner resolve had been stripped from me.

Meeka crawled to the blade of silver grass. She laughed. Tiny eyes gazed between us and her creation. She beamed with pride.

"Look, Mack." I stood up. "She can't go. What does "special home" even mean? She needs us, not strangers."

"Bababen," Meeka gurgled something and the rug vanished from under our feet.

Mack gave me his "I told you so" look.

"It's probably just oxygen or nitrogen," I said reassuring myself as much as him.

Mack stepped back as if he was scared of our daughter. "We'll have to watch her every second for her safety. And ours. You'll have to give up your job. People will ask why?
The settler's soldiers will find out."

"I don't care. My baby's special. She's not like the other Terras. We are going to look after her as long as possible." Terras. I can't believe I'd said that disgusting word. Did that make me a bad mother? Everybody knew it was a derogatory term for the Elementals and everybody still used it, but what kind of person would use it to describe their own baby? She wasn't a terror. She was sweet and bubbly and the most beautiful thing on this planet. She was special.

"Come on, Sherie." Mack grabbed my arm and pulled me close so he could whisper in my ear. "It won't be long before people notice our rug transformed. We have to go."

Meeka gazed up at the tree in the middle of the bio-dome. The bare-branched tree had been the first one the settlers planted. The seed sprouted and then blossomed and then it just gave up the ghost: leaves fell, bark stripped away. It never recovered, despite the garden's increasingly fertile soil. Despite its withered greying branches it was a tribute, it was a statue to all we'd been through during the terraforming process. It meant something to all of us, and my baby was pointing her tiny finger towards it.

"An-"

Mack cupped his hand over her mouth, silencing her. "No!" he yelled at her.

I snatched her up. "No, not that tree, sweetie. Please!"

The family nearby stood abruptly. The mother gave me *that* look. I'd seen it before Meeka was born. Back at the camps, another mother was trying to stop her son from turning the parent's food rations into lead.

The father turned to the guards at the entrance of the bio-dome. He clicked his fingers. "Hey!" he yelled. "There's a Terra over here."

The guard turned in our direction.

"There's no evidence. They can't prove anything," I whispered. "We should just go back to our quarters."

The guard approached, tapping his baton against his leg.

"Forget the basket." I grabbed Mack's hand.

"Wait!" yelled the guard.

"We can't run. They could look after her in the home." There was a trace of doubt in Mack's voice. Deep down, he had to know there was something wrong with that place.

"I don't trust them," I whispered to him. "They say they train them and we've all seen the displays by adult Elementals where they conjure titanium and copper, but why..." I chocked on my words as the guard stopped by the father and his two rowdy sons. They exchanged words.

I took a deep breath to recover. "Why do they not help terraform the land beyond the Seam? They could create bridges and rich soil everywhere, instead they just make more weapons for those in the domes. And the camps don't change. The terraforming has stopped, but my baby ... all the Elementals ... they could help," my voice sunk to a whisper as the guard approached us. "The settler's soldiers could do so much. She's our daughter, Mack."

He held up a finger to his lips silencing me.

"Please listen, we can look after her," I pleaded.

"Hello." The soldier addressed us pleasantly enough with a nod and smile.

"These people here," he turned back to the family and gave them a nod, "tell me your baby may be a Terra."

"Elemental," I corrected. "But no, she's normal." Normal. I was still using these kinds of words about my own baby. Doubt crept in; it had been lurking deep down. In that tiny place of my brain I didn't want to address, I knew my baby wasn't normal. I shook my head. What kind of mother was I? She was special. She was the most special thing on this forsaken planet. "Elementals are normal by the way," I yelled.

The guard must have detected the sudden defiance in my voice. His eyes widened. "Of course they are." He touched my baby's nose delicately.

I wanted to clobber his patronising mouth.

"But," the guard continued his voice harshening again, "they must be registered and the special home caters for their needs." He tapped his baton against his leg. Tap, tap, tap.

I wanted to snatch it and beat him over his podgy head. What was this fat menace eating? Even in the bio-domes food was scarce. Maybe that was what they used the Elementals for, conjuring food and weapons solely for the settler's soldiers.

"It's for everyone's safety, including yours and your baby's," he said.

I turned to Mack and caught his eye. "She's our baby," I mouthed the words, hoping the guard didn't catch on to my desperation. "We can look after her." There was still doubt lingering inside me, but I didn't care how hard it was, we could make it work.

"They will keep her safe." The guard tapped his baton again, stronger and more menacing.

"I'm sure they do." Mack turned away from me back to the guard. I prayed I'd gotten through to him, but his voice was so calm. He clasped Meeka's tiny foot dangling by my side and smiled at her. "I'm sure they do a great job. But our baby is perfect."

"Really?" The guard swung his baton up and tapped it against his palm.

"Yes. She is perfect." I hugged her close. That wasn't a lie. She was the most perfect thing ever.

"If you say so." The guard didn't sound convinced. "I don't blame you. We don't fully understand the effect the Seam has during pregnancy, some people just don't heed the warnings. But for everyone's safety-"

"It's not her fault!" Mack yelled.

"I didn't say—"

"You implied it, you arrogant fat monster." I'd never seen Mack so worked up. "She is our perfect Elemental and we can look after her ourselves."

The guard put his baton back in its holster and reached out, grabbing Meeka by the waist. "I'm afraid you don't have a choice."

I held on tight.

"You need to register and comply with Settlement Law."

"You need to back off." Mack pushed him away.

"I don't want to force you." The guard took out his baton again.

"Barbon." Meeka turned to the guard and smiled. "Barbon."

His baton turned to soot and sprinkled onto the soil and grass.

"Barbentum." She looked at Mack. That was how Meeka had said Argentum before, but nothing changed, nothing materialised.

Mack suddenly smiled. "Soot is a good thing. Adds carbon to the soil." He lifted up the picnic basket. "It might even mean less stale bread."

"What?" Without his baton the soldier's confidence fell like the fallen ash.

Mack swung the picnic basket sideways and thwacked it into the side of the guard's head. He tumbled to the ground, groaning.

Mack placed the picnic basket down and pulled out the loaf of bread. "You are a beautiful little thing aren't you?" He kissed Meeka's cheek, and unravelled the cloth revealing a rectangular lump of silver. He took the transformed loaf and clubbed the guard again. "Go!"

I didn't hesitate. I ran past the family standing under the monument tree. The parents said nothing, but I caught a fleeting glance. The mother's wrinkled up face and narrowed eyes didn't seem angry or fearful, there was sympathy, pity even. Would I get that look if I managed to keep her safe and hidden in the camps? An adult could control their gift, but children were unpredictable. Would people be fearful and turn on her?

I shook my head trying to clear the thought. That could wait for later, all that mattered now was keeping her out of the authority's hands. I punched the release button on the doors of the bio-dome just as an alarm sounded. A spinning light flashed red above the sliding door. I glanced back.

"Mack!"

He sprinted from the guard sprawled on the floor. The monotonous beep drowned out my voice. The doors began to close. Once we left, they'd never let us back in the domes. It had taken us so long to work our way up here. I looked at Meeka's beaming eyes. It was worth it. I stepped outside.

"Hurry, Mack!" The gap between the sliding door and the wall narrowed. A metre. Half a metre. Ten centimetres. It shut just as Mack reached it.

I slapped my hand on the door. I clasped my fingers on the edge and tried to pull. There was no way I could look after her without him. I rested my forehead against it. "Can you get out another way!" I yelled.

"No, there are guards coming. Just go."

"No. I can't."

"Barbon."

I fell forwards as black soot rained down on my hair and on Mack's. He stood wide-eyed.

"My beautiful little genius." He kissed Meeka leaving sooty lip marks on her cheek.

She truly was special, developmentally way beyond her years. She looked up at me and rested her tiny head against my chest.

Mack took my hand. "Come on."

We turned to see at least two dozen beggars from the camps protesting outside. They held placards asking for food, asking for justice, asking for equality. A jumble of expressions shone from the crowd: confusion, pity, fear...

"We understand," Mack addressed them. "We came from the camps."

I turned back. The guards weren't far behind. At least five of them ran towards the door, wielding guns. They wouldn't shoot on a baby, even if she was an Elemental. Surely?

One of the beggars approached. He lowered his placard and walked past us. He rested his hand on Mack's shoulder and gave him a look I didn't understand.

Mack must've understood though, as he whispered, "thank you."

The rest of the crowd strode towards the door. One tore the sign off his placard leaving just a hefty stick. He grasped it in his hand like a baton. Others followed his lead.

Mack grabbed my free hand and led me away. I couldn't quite fathom what we just witnessed. Were they just using the opportunity to invade the bio-domes, or were they defending my baby, my clearly different baby? I clutched her tight at my side. She made a string of indistinguishable gurgling sounds in my ear. Logically, I should have been concerned, but in my heart, I knew she wouldn't hurt me. It was as if she knew what she was doing, which sounded ridiculous, but my special girl was so smart.

As we darted towards the camps, I glanced back. The glass bio-domes stood like monolithic statues. Inside there might be greenery and thriving communities, but there was something lifeless and fake about them from here.

Ahead of us, the beige tents dotted the rocky landscape, beyond that the green strip of the Seam was just visible.

I took one last look through the glass of the bio-dome. The grass and vegetables surrounded the Monument Tree standing proudly in the middle. Meeka loved all that. It wasn't ideal, but we could survive out here in the camps again.

The relative shelter of the camps gave us some reprieve and we slowed our pace, strolling down an alley filled with trestle tables selling nutrient sachets and other remnant supplies from the first settlers. Sheep hides from the stock, which the first settlers cloned, hung from hooks by the tents. The odd piece of fruit scavenged from the Seam dotted the tables. The Elementals could do so much here. Yet they weren't out in the fields adding nitrogen and phosphorus to the soil. Crops planted near the Seam were rank and had failed to set seed. It still only rained a few times a year. Were the Elementals trained, or just contained? Any confusion I might have had vanished. There was no way my baby was going to a home.

Mack's grip on my hand suddenly tightened. I followed his gaze. Soldiers patrolled the alleyway up ahead. He pulled me down a side alley.

A makeshift hospital, which was nothing more than an open tent with mattresses salvaged from the ships, was full of patients. A frail skinny baby sat on a mat near us, attached to a bag of fluid running into its veins. It stared up with sunken eyes. I'd forgotten how bad it was out here. Livestock with concave flanks, ambled in pens made from scraps of tin from the ships.

We kept walking further and further from the heart of the camps to the Seam. Here, at the chasm where the terraforming started, we could hide between the few denuded trees, but it wasn't much shelter and wouldn't hide us for long.

I stopped at a grove of small pine trees that poked through cracks in the black igneous rock. They were one of the few things they'd been able to establish away from the bio-domes. Pine needles lay underneath barely decomposed. I sat Meeka down on them. She picked one up and studied it, tasted it, and spat it out again.

"We can't stop here long," said Mack. "They'll eventually work out where we've fled."

Stomping of heavy boots on rocky ground and shouting drifted through the trees.

"They can't have found us already."

Was this what life was going to be like? Running, fleeing, fearing. Every day.

In the distance, a dozen soldiers stormed towards us, blocking the path back to the camp.

Mack picked up Meeka. "Head to the footbridge."

Was that the best idea? There was no shelter on the other side of the chasm, the ground was rockier, the terraformed soil even thinner. But at this point in time, I couldn't think of any better solutions.

The rope bridge traversed the twenty-metre ravine below. It waved in the gentle breeze like a children's swing.

When we lived in the camps, few were game enough to make the crossing. Those that did might find the odd blackberry bush or milk thistle. Beyond that small strip of greenery were the signs. The same ones they had the other side of the bio-domes warning people not to venture further.

It looked harmless enough, but it was an inhospitable wasteland away from the terraformed region of the Seam.

Mack passed Meeka to me. He tested his weight on the wooden planks, stepping tentatively, and keeping his eyes focused ahead instead of the long drop below.

"It's okay," he said after a few paces.

I held Meeka tight and followed him. Unlike Mack, I couldn't help but look down. The bottom wasn't visible, but straggly plants grew from the sides. A few pigeons that the first settler's had cloned, even clung to an overhang of ragged rock and cooed. I always wondered what was down there before the first settlers initiated their terraforming device in the chasm. It was so deep. Surely nothing could live in that dark place or with the lack of oxygen the planet had before we landed. Even if nothing lived down there, I liked to think it went all the way to the planet's heart.

"Halt!"

I'd almost forgotten about the soldiers. I stopped looking down and quickened my pace.

"For your own safety ... and hers ... we command you to stop." The guard who spoke actually had concern in his voice.

Carefully, I turned, avoiding the cracks in the planks below me.

"Good, now I need you to pin her lips together with your fingers." The guard demonstrated by grabbing his own lips.

"What? No!" I held her tight and took a tentative step backwards towards Mack who had reached the other side.

"Listen to me. You are on a bridge over a drop that is so long that no one has ever measured it. You are on a bridge with an Elemental."

He didn't say Terra. For a split second, I almost trusted his words, but then Mack's reassuring voice cut through all the political spin.

"Nothing has changed. If they don't think her own parents can look after her, then how do they control the elementals?

"You've seen the exhibitions. We have proven techniques to help them."

"What, staple their mouths shut until they are old enough to do your bidding? And how do you make them obey?" Mack's voice was harsh. I'd never heard him so passionate. His voice softened as he addressed me. "She is our daughter. Remember? We are both confused, but like you said we'll work this out ourselves. Don't trust them. Trust your instincts."

"For Seam's sake, she is a baby. You can't control her. She needs to be trained." The guard took a step on the bridge.

"Amama," Meeka babbled in her cooing voice.

I gasped and tightened my grip on the rope with my free hand. We hadn't fallen, but an illogical part of my brain checked that the bridge was still intact under my feet. On either side of the chasm, the rocks still stood like normal dull rocks. The settler's soldier squad still brandished normal steel blades and batons. Like me, they were all glancing around, wondering what she had conjured or changed.

The ground trembled.

Mack raced down the bridge towards me. He grabbed my hand. Dozens of pigeons flew up out of the Seam in a myriad of directions. Their wings created enough breeze to blow my hair across my eyes.

"What's going on?" I was hugging Meeka so tight I was scared I would suffocate her.

"Anima," Meeka's voice was clearer this time, but it still sounded like baby-talk. I blew the hair from my eyes. Nothing had changed.

"This is your last chance," bellowed a different soldier. "We will take her without your consent if it comes to that." Were they playing good cop, bad cop?

"Come and get her then." Mack gripped my hand tighter and started walking.

"Anima."

I could feel the bridge beneath my feet and my baby in my arms. If anything else had changed, I didn't care.

The ground trembled again. The bridge swayed more vigorously. I couldn't help but look down into the Seam as we walked. Something furry was crawling up the side. My heart pounded in my chest. I wanted to run but was so fearful I'd trip and drop Meeka.

I heard the creaking of wooden planks as the podgy soldiers made their way across behind us. Mack pulled himself up on the other side. I passed Meeka to him. Panting, on hands and knees, I crawled off the bridge onto the rocky ground. Although it wasn't rocky. A green carpet crept over the edge of the chasm under my knees. For a split second, I thought Meeka might have conjured some toxic sludge, until I peered closer. Little cotyledon seedlings poked through the soil. Soil! Thick dark brown soil. One by one, the green seedlings popped up like spears, covering the ground.

"Oh, you are special aren't you, my beautiful darling girl." Mack spun Meeka around and kissed her forehead.

"Anima," she mumbled again.

I stood. It wasn't a type of element. At least none that I was aware of.

Mack must've seen my confused expression. "Ancient Earth language," he whispered.

"For what?"

"Soul." He grabbed my hand. "We should go while they are distracted."

I hadn't noticed the soldiers, but they stood in awe, gazing in every direction as the greenery ran over the barren wastelands.

"Go where?" I whispered.

Mack shrugged and pointed to the landscape transforming before our eyes. "Wherever we want."

Above us, the sky suddenly darkened. Clouds crackled and a hefty drop of water fell on the back of my neck.

"Anima." Meeka beamed with pride.

"Yes, Mummy thinks you're a good girl." I kissed her cheek and we strode towards the desolate lands beyond with the green carpet following our heels.

I always knew my baby was special.

Pre-emptive

Against the fading light, the silhouetted shapes look like harmless cardboard cut-outs pasted against the sky. But these shapes are one-dimensional caricatures of something more foreboding, portentously suspended high above the planet's surface, lingering, waiting for a second onslaught — or something more sinister.

I race towards the impact area, trying not to dwell on the imminent threat above. Radiant heat from the ruined city stews my skin, but I pelt along the alleys, through rubble-strewn streets, holding onto a glimpse of hope that she has survived. Long gone are the welcoming parties, standing on rooftops, inviting the newcomers with placards and cheers of jubilation. Frivolity has waned to futility, crowds of onlookers replaced with corpses, and cheers displaced by the consternated cries of fleeing survivors.

I speed around a corner, but my flight is cut short by the river. The bridge is barely intact. Yet I see her, lying on the other side, limp and motionless.

Tentatively, I balance my weight on the remaining frail structure. It creaks ominously. A dark torrent is visible between the bridge's slats. Don't look down, don't look down. Giddy and nauseous, I near the other side. Almost there...

But it is not to be. There is a twang. A strand of rope snaps and the bridge plummets.

Hands forward, I break my fall, landing in the shallows. Hypnotic ripples ruffle the river's surface. Shivers creep along my spine.

I stagger backwards, out of the river, and collide with something solid.

Two menacing, foreign beings tower over me. Horrific aliens, strangely similar, yet nothing like us at the same time. Two arms, two legs, torso and head.

One of the aliens points a smooth metallic stick at my head. I peer along its tubular barrel at an unknown fear, shudder, and cast my eye briefly towards my beloved. If only I could distract them and bide her time to escape. Oh please get up, please, please, please. I wait for the worst. Nothing happens.

The being looks at my hands. Frozen, I watch a vile, pink fleshy appendage grasp my wrist, wiping off sticky, black river remains.

Eventually, it lets go and I scramble to cradle my beloved. I feel the base of her tail. A pulse. Relieved, I arouse her.

Her eye opens, warily.

Nearby, ignoring my escape, the alien rubs black river fluid between two digits. The other alien stares with upturned mouth. Awestruck, they peer past us to the viscous river, Aruh, snaking its way into the mountains.

Lights shine from the spaceships above and hordes of aliens descend in shuttles. I hold my beloved's clammy blue hand. We embrace, and watch.

The brutish aliens hoist huge containers out of the shuttles and enthusiastically scoop up gallons of black fluid. They disturb the perilous river, the ripples sending messages deep below.

Silently, we slide away into the numinous night.

Looking back, I see the oily river swirl as the monstrous serpent Aruh surfaces from the riverbed — her pursed lips and viper tongue hungry for new blood.

Time to kill

There was a wrong and a right, but as Jordan looked at the glimmer in Ella's eyes, he started to question whether The Agency knew which was which.

"Come on, Jordan. It's over here." Ella walked under the old Oak, her hair shining in the moonlight.

Jordan peered at the tree with its auburn leaves clinging desperately to the braches, trying to avoid falling into the River Aran.

"See, I told you it was beautiful."

In the moonlight, the rippling water shimmered.

"Yes it is." He met her gaze.

Ella smiled and reached for his hand. He flinched.

"What's wrong?" She reached out again.

"Ella, there are things you don't know."

"I know all I need to –"

"I'm not from this place... this... time."

"I... don't understand." She wrapped her sweater around her as a wind stirred the leaves in the canopy.

For the first time in his career he felt the need to justify himself. Pull yourself together Jordan, it's just a job. Like any other. "What I do is for the greater good, for the future good of society. The Time Agency, they know what they are doing. Future terrorists, dictators, they are only people who will harm those in my time." He touched the revolver inside jacket, but as he looked at her wide glimmering eyes, he couldn't bring himself to pull it.

"Ella... I... the Agency know what's best. They... you..." he choked on the words.

He looked away towards the river. "In training they tell us to get close enough to do the job, but not so close that..." He looked back towards her and instantly regretted it, the night's veil didn't conceal her face and he saw the glimmer in her eyes fade.

She took a step back. "Wha... But... We..."

Her reaction was too slow. He blocked her punch and with one swift move spun her around clasping her neck. Her feeble body no match for his two strong arms. Her gasps lasted seconds.

A portal of light pierced the sky and a dark figure from The Agency walked out of the shadows. "Well done. The Agency has another assignment in this same time. You'll be given details soon."

"I know we shouldn't ask, but what was she going to do? I hardly picture her as a terrorist."

"She would have had a wise man's child." The man spoke in riddles.

Jordan shrugged. "What was this child going to do then?"

"You don't want to know." The agent started to walk back to the portal.

Jordan tugged the agents black coat. "Wait! You have to tell me."

The anonymous agent stood motionless. "I'm risking my life telling you."

"Please," begged Jordan.

"The child would have stirred something in the father." His voice was ruthlessly steady. "Prevented him from killing again. Prevented him from doing his next assignment."

Jordan stood for a moment and then it sunk in. He crumpled to his knees, cradling the pieces of his future valentine under the tree.

Timely drop

Nestled amongst used pizza boxes and Jack's office work, sat another empty wine bottle. He must've found this one in the back of the cellar, as it was dusty and the label with its intricate gold lettering was peeling off. And like always Jack left it for me to clean up. Was he really drinking instead of dealing with our marital problems, or was he leaving rubbish lying around solely to grind at my patience? How hard was it to put in the recycling bin? Pick up bottle, open bin lid, place bottle in bin.

Well, I wasn't cleaning up for him this time. I strolled down the hallway. His snoring echoed from the bedroom as if leading the way.

His legs splayed diagonally across the mattress, taking up both his and my side of the bed. I pushed him until he rolled over. A subdued groan escaped his lips. I flicked on the bedside light, hoping it would wake him and stop him snoring.

"What you doing?" He grumbled and sat up.

"Reading." I quickly picked up my book.

"Do you have to read now?"

"I don't know. Do you have to snore and leave your empty wine bottles and rubbish everywhere?"

"Huh? What bottle?"

"On the kitchen table."

"It wasn't mine." He snuggled back down and shut his eyes.

"Well it doesn't have legs. It couldn't have walked up from the cellar and emptied itself."

"Do we have to start arguing now, Dear?" he snapped.

"Don't you "Dear" me, Honey." I opened my book and pretended to read. What had happened to us? We were so in love once. The words danced on the page, blurring behind a thin veil of tears.

Part of me longed for Jack to ask what was wrong, but the other part was relieved he was lying on his back snoring like a cranky lawnmower already.

I put the book back on my bedside table. As I did so, the walls shimmered pale blue. I switched off the lamp, but the light remained.

"Jack!" I shook his shoulders, but he just snorted at me.

I reached for the lamp again and hit something hard, sending it crashing to the floor.

Jack woke with a start. "What's wrong now?"

I ignored him and stood without thinking. Sharp pain pierced the sole of my foot and I let out a shriek that would have woken the whole neighbourhood.

Jack sprung out of bed like a springtail jumping from a puddle. "Are you okay?"

"No." I bit my tongue as I inspected a smashed wine bottle on the floor and drops of blood on my plush carpet.

Jack ran to the on suite and returned with a towel. He sat beside me, wrapping my foot in one of our expensive Egyptian cotton towels. But as he put pressure on the wound and nestled beside me I forgot about that, his quirks, and all his mess. It had been so long since I felt comforted like this.

He leant over the side of the bed and picked up the neck of the bottle with its jagged edge.

"What were you doing with this?"

"I didn't put it there." Something poked out of the neck of the bottle. "What's that?" I pulled out a tiny scroll of crisp brown paper.

"Why are you asking me?" Just like that, that moment of affection between us had gone. He snatched the paper from my hands and unfurled it. "S.O.S. I'm stranded. Please help," he read. "Did you find this at the beach or something?" he asked.

"I didn't put it there!"

The room shimmered blue again. Jack looked to the ceiling lights, probably thinking the same as I was, but they weren't flickering or faltering.

A blue flash above the dresser caught my eye. My eyes adjusted to the light to find another bottle of wine.

"Did you see that?" asked Jack, leaving me to walk to the dresser.

Although he couldn't see me, I nodded. "

He picked up the bottle and inspected the label. "2030 vintage," he read. "Is that meant to be a joke?"

He pulled out another tiny scroll with golden edging.

"S.O.S. Something happened with you guys. I'm stranded in a deserted segment of time." Jack looked as confused by the message as I felt.

"Twenty thirty, that's just..." began Jack.

"...crazy," I finished his sentence.

My mind raced to the bottle in the kitchen. "The bottle in the kitchen, are you sure it wasn't yours?"

"Positive." Jack caught onto my train of thought and raced to the kitchen. He returned moments later with the bottle. "There's no note sticking out," he said, his voice deflated.

"What about inside?" I asked.

Jack peered down the nozzle. "I see it." He tipped it upside down and shook until a tiny slip of pale pink paper fell on the mattress.

Neither of us read it aloud. It just seemed too ludicrous.'

"S.O.S. Please, don't give up. Chill and have a drink for me, Mum and Dad." I read the note. I know Jack had read it too. His eyes grew wide and there was the faintest hint of a smile.

My hand rested on my stomach. Children were the last thing on our mind now, but a few months ago, we had tried.

"I guess I should clean up this mess," said Jack, looking at the broken glass and bloodstain on the carpet.

"It can wait." I threw the message from the bottle on the floor too, grabbed Jack by the collar of his pyjamas and pulled him close.

The Dragon

Smell comes first, a reek like decaying fish, wafting towards me through the black. Pinpricks in my legs and a sensation of liquid running through my veins. Amid the haziness of recollection, my brain manages to draw conclusions. I can feel. I can smell.

I still am.

A metallic voice speaks. "Emergency power critical. Thawing complete."

The words should have meaning, but they seem muddled. It matters not. Words can wait. I still am. How I still am, I do not know.

I lift my hands and feel the lid of a casket. The cryo casket. They've woken me. Is it possible? Could there be a cure?

The metallic voice recedes – drawn out like a record played too slow – then dies altogether.

A new voice echoes in the dark. "We gotta hurry. Backup generator's clapped out. I refuelled. Lights should kick in soon, but the fuel won't last long."

A circle of light penetrates the darkness. It skitters over the lid of the clear casket as my weary arms manage to push the lid ajar.

Light shines on my face. There is a gasp and a different voice – mousy, not metallic. "Marco," it whispers. "Is he..."

Another circle of light appears. It approaches like a firefly fluttering closer and closer.

There's a whirr and click. Lights flicker on in the room and I'm staring into a crossbow.

A man holds the weapon with gloved hands: surgical gloves. He lowers his face closer. Mouth obscured by green cloth mask. Maybe I'm no longer at the cryogenics. A doctor? They must be administering the cure. Then I remember the crossbow and confusion sets in.

"His eyes are clear," says the masked man. "He's paisley though. Is anaemia an early symptom?"

"Are you clean?" asks the owner of the mousy voice. She is small, just a child – thirteen at most. Like the older male, her mouth is covered by a surgical mask; hands are gloved; eyes are wide. "Are you clean?" she repeats more urgently.

"What? I don't..." I catch the strangulation in my voice — the harsh guttural tones and crackling from my throat cancer. So do they.

"Staggers!" The man loads a quarrel in his crossbow and takes a step backwards ready to fire.

"Wait!" I rasp, clutching at my throat.

The man's fingers tremble as he aims the quarrel at my head.

"Marcus, wait! He doesn't look like he's got Schtager's disease." The girl lowers the torch and moves closer, keeping cautious. "Who are you?"

"Sean." I clutch my throat. "Cancer."

She shrugs.

"It was a disease," says Marcus.

"Was?" I glare at the man. "Then where's my cure?"

He doesn't respond, instead he lowers his mask and turns to the girl. "It's okay, Tina. I think he's clean."

"You sure?" she whispers, pulling her own mask down.

Marcus nods and pays me no further notice. He opens a rucksack and strips the cryo's shelves of bottles of sterile water, facemasks and alcohol swabs. "Rope?" he asks.

"Can't hurt," Tina replies. She's still staring at me as Marcus throws the items in his rucksack.

I swing my legs over the side of the casket. They dangle and blood returns to my limbs. Nausea radiates throughout my stomach. "Hey!" I call out. "Where's my cure?" I paid millions. I've waited.

Marcus just grunts and opens a freezer. "You think this ice is safe?" he asks Tina, but she doesn't respond.

I try to stand. My legs buckle and bile rises up my oesophagus. I clasp the side of the cryopreservation casket to steady myself. As I do so, I notice the console has been smashed. No wonder I'm awake. On the far side of the room, sits another casket, its lid pulverised, the body inside cold blue. Why would they do this? I look at Tina. She returns my gaze with big green eyes.

"We can't leave him here."

Marcus snorts. "Wanna bet? He's slow and arrogant. He'll get us killed. Or worse."

Why would Marcus smash the console then wake me up? And if he didn't destroy it, then who did?

"I remember a few months back someone had a sharp tongue and broken foot." Tina smiles at Marcus.

He grunts at me. "Come on then. I ain't waiting though." He turns toward the stairs that lead to the door.

I look down at my white linen gown. "Where's my suit? My phone? Access to my bank accounts. At the very least, I need a suit on my back. It was an Armani," I try to explain.

Marcus slings the rucksack on his shoulders. "Bleeding heck, who is this nut job-"

The lights flicker out.

"Is that the generator?" asks Tina.

Footsteps echo in this distance, clomping along a corridor with methodical rhythm.

"Go," whispers Marcus.

Tina grabs my arm and helps me along.

I struggle to maintain her pace. My legs burn as I stagger up the stairs. Stumbling blindly in the dark, I stub my toes, but she guides me. Up ahead, a sliver of light indicates the outside world. The door is close. Just a few more agonising steps.

"How far is the nearest hospital?" I ask. "Do you think they'll be able to cure me?"

Light plays upon Marcus's features and I catch him rolling his eyes as he pushes the door with his shoulder.

My eyes find it difficult to adjust to daylight.

Tina hands me a facemask. "Don't touch anything or interact with anyone. The water's still infected with Schtager's disease." She speaks quickly. As my eyes adjust to the brightness I realise she holds a dagger in one hand and makeshift spear in the other. "As if infecting the water wasn't enough, last year they dropped a gene bomb directly over the city." Her eyes glance from side to side. "I've no doubt your genome's susceptible." She looks up with her big green eyes as if expecting some kind of response.

"Huh?" The mumbo jumbo streams over the top of my head.

"Tina, I don't think he's been outside for quite some time," says Marcus. He turns to me. "Basically, don't drink from the taps and if you see someone who looks sick – run."

"Run?"

Marcus nods, looks me up and down and smiles. "Or walk… as quickly as you can, in your state."

Confused, I glance at my surrounds. Sunlight catches the mist lingering in the air leaving an orange hue over the horizon. My eyes begin to focus. It's not mist but smoke billowing from burnt-out buildings and rubble-strewn streets. Ahead, a gaping hole has been ripped through a skyscraper. Steel cables dangle from exposed floors like entrails.

"The hospital?" My mind focusses on one thing. I can't die. Not now. I've waited so long and if there is any chance of a cure…

"The government's genetic munitions factory might-"

"What!" Marcus lowers his crossbow and turns to Tina. "You can't be serious. You'd risk the wrath of The Dragon to help this guy?

She gazes up at Marcus – a foot taller than she is. "If we can't help others, we are no better than *them*. You should know better than anyone what–"

Whirring helicopter blades drown out her tirade. Behind me, there is a crash and splinters of wood ricochet into the back of my naked knees.

"Staggers!" yells Marcus.

A man blocks the doorway to the cryopreservation centre. His face is pale, the whites of his eyes are stained a sickly yellow. He stumbles, making his way through the shattered doorframe, those yellow eyes aimed at us. "Hrp."

"What?" His voice is even more guttural than mine.

Tina grabs my wrist and pulls me back. "You can't help him. The disease attacks the frontal lobe. They don't know what they're doing, or what they're saying. They don't feel. They just hallucinate."

"Gurblins. Prixies." He tumbles forward. His knee splits open on a rock and blood spurts across the cracked pavement. "Grp. Snks. You see." The man claws at his shattered knee, pulling at loose tendons.

My stomach churns. Just as I'm about to hurl, shrill whistling sounds, streaming like a gust of wind through a canyon. Above me, missiles fly towards the helicopter.

"Down!"

Someone pulls me to the ground. My knees buckle as the sky explodes above.

I'm overcome by a chalky stench. Dust smothers my medical gown and legs. I sit up, shaking it off.

Lying on the ground beside me, Marcus grabs my arm. "The government, they're all for the good of the nation, but rarely the good of the people. The enemy sends bombs, our government sends some back. It's never ending. They need someone to help them see things clearly. Perhaps see things from a more *innocent* point of view." He looks at me intently and then at Tina. "You understand what I'm saying? If you go to the munitions factory, make them see. She could make them see."

Stupid fool. I wrench my arm free of Marcus's grip. He rolls over panting.

"Marcus!" Tina's high-pitch scream resonates between the desolate buildings. Furiously, she shakes dust from her hair and rips out alcohol swabs, cleaning her skin.

"It's okay," says Marcus. "It's just a regular bomb."

"You sure?" The doubt in her voice evident.

"Just a bomb. We could have died." What is wrong with these people?

Giddy, I stand to survey the destruction. The diseased man lies amongst the rubble. His elbow is bent at an impossibly obtuse angle, a rivulet of blood trickles from a gash on his temple. "Grp. Goblin," he mumbles. He rolls onto his side and pummels his fists into the pavement until his knucklebones protrude through the skin. With a bony hand, he reaches out to grasp Marcus's leg. "Gurblin. Hrp. Kill."

Marcus shrieks in pain as the man's bloody fingernails dig into his shin.

Tina lunges, grabs the crossbow from the ground and fires at the diseased man. "Wash it! Clean it out," she yells at Marcus, pelting him with alcohol swabs and water.

Marcus stares at his leg, eyes wide.

I pull Tina back. "We can't do anything. We have to get the genetic munitions factory." Who knows how long I have left before the cancer takes over completely.

"No! We can't leave Marcus," she cries.

You want to bet. I snatch the crossbow from her unresisting hands and point it at her.

"What? I don't..." she stumbles over her words.

"We keep moving." *I still am. I still need to be. Nothing is going to stand in my way.*

Marcus looks at her with misty eyes. "The sky is swirling." He extends an arm and touches the air. "It's quite quick." He looks at the crossbow in my hand. "Please."

"No," cries Tina. "We'll find help at The Dragon."

Marcus shakes his head. "You know what you have to do."

Tina clasps my arm. "Don't."

He'll hold us up. I'll never make it to the munitions factory. I take aim.

Tina turns away and starts sobbing.

I discharge the crossbow at close range. My aim is slightly off, but the result is still effective. He falls onto his back, gasps and then gasps no more.

"No!" Tina slumps to her knees.

I grab Marcus's rucksack. "Come on."

Tina gets to her feet and grabs her weapons like it's a reflex action, but the resolve she had in her eyes is no longer there.

We wander down the street and for a few minutes Tina seems to have regained her composure, but soon she starts crying. Her sobs become drawn out, painful wails of grief. She screams Marcus's name.

I catch a flicker of movement in an adjacent ruin. Just shadows? "You need to be quiet," I tell her.

It's too late. An infected person staggers into view. With unsteady gait, it lurches towards us from the ruins.

I continue as fast as I can, but my legs are still unsteady and the ground is littered with broken concrete. I stumble. My legs don't seem to find the strength to stand again. A few feet away a diseased woman mumbles in indiscernible tones.

Tina is suddenly by my side. After all she has been through, she still comes back to help me. She drags me to my feet, puts an arm around my waist and pulls me forward.

We put distance between us and the diseased man. A mix of weariness and nausea radiate through me, but Tina won't let me rest. Shadows grow long as the sun passes its zenith and begins its descent to the horizon. Tina helps me pluck my way through the rubble but she doesn't speak until we come to the end of the city and start our way up a long hill.

"I know you were just trying to save us, but we could have helped him," she eventually says.

Was I trying to help? Let her think that, so long as we make it to the munitions factory there is still a chance I will be okay.

"Okay, maybe we couldn't have helped him." She obviously takes my lack or response to mean something else. "But..." Her voice trails off.

"Did you not have someone? Before you went into the cryo thing. Did you not have anyone in your life to care for?"

"I had a wife and two children."

Her mouth falls open. "And you left them alone?"

"I was going to die anyway."

"There are worse things than death," she says. Her words are as pointed as the spear in her hands.

"I was going to die." I don't know why I'm bothering to justify myself but for some reason I need her to understand. "I spent all my life working ridiculous hours, building up my business and what for? I can't die. Not now."

She looks at my torso. The medical gown – she probably doesn't realise what a successful man I am... I was.

"There really is nothing inside there, is there?" she says, her eyes boring a hole into my chest. Turning on her heel, she continues up the hill not waiting for me to catch her up.

When I finally reach the top, there is a sheer drop before me. In the valley below sits the remains of what might have once been a town. Tina perches on a rock, knees pressed close against her body. She stares out at the ruinous landscape as the sun begins to melt into the land.

"There it is." She points toward the plain below. "The Dragon. Isn't it beautiful?"

Beautiful? Dragon? There's rubble and tents surrounded by a razor wire fence – nothing but a desolate hole. Could there really be enough technology in there to save me?

"You see it?" she asks, beaming proudly. "The Dragon? Look for it."

"You sure you're not infected and hallucinating?"

She ignores my jibe. "See, the former oval is its body. The rubble from the old defence station curves around like the tail. See how the army tents glisten and shimmer in the fading light, like dragon scales."

"Huh?" I mutter. She is clearly nuts.

"And the electric gate makes the mouth."

"Electric? Great. So how do we get in?"

"You really can't see it?" She sounds so disappointed.

I see ruins. But I also see a chance that they might hold a cure with their genetic research so I just shrug. "How do we get down there?"

"They don't take kindly to outsiders. It's likely the gate will be guarded, especially at night. We should wait "til morning, go back down the hill and wave a white flag as we approach, I guess."

"You guess." I'm too tired to argue. "You keep first watch then. I'm shattered."

She doesn't object. Instead, she pulls out her knife and spear and looks across the plains at the rubble where I hope to find salvation. I settle down, lying uncomfortably on the stony hillside, slowly drifting into uneasy slumber.

Next thing I know, Tina's shaking me awake. A dozen infected people are staggering up the hillside. "Can we run past them?" I ask. Even as I say the words, I know it's futile. "What about the rope?" But there are no trees, no stumps, no large stones to loop a rope around.

She reaches the same conclusion. "I can hold the rope. You climb down."

"Okay." The staggers are closing in on us. I'm not going to argue.

She wraps the rope around her midriff. "I think I can take your weight. You need to go now," she says, glancing back down the hill.

It doesn't take me long to realise there is no way she can do it. I'm twice her size. She braces herself, heels digging into the soil as I tug on the rope to test its strength. In desperation, I examine the cliff face. Maybe I could climb down. A bad idea. I can barely walk. It hits me with gusto. I am going to die.

"I'll try again," she says, gritting her teeth.

I know it's no use and so does she.

"I can defend you." She steps forward, her spear thrust forward, shaking slightly.

I turn around looking for a rock or something I could use as a weapon. I'm so close. I can't die now. But in the soft dusk light there's nothing to see. Nothing but The Dragon encampment below. A couple of lights flicker on in one of the run-down buildings, the one right next to the gate or the *mouth* as Tina calls it. Light means people. There might still be a chance.

"You go." I take the rope from her and wrap it around my waist.

"No." She shakes her head. "I can't go on alone again. Please," she begs in her mousy voice.

"You won't be alone. There are people in there – go to them." I secure the rope with a double knot. "Go now – and get me help."

She passes me the spear. "I'll be quick."

I nod as she grabs the rope and disappears over the edge. I can barely feel her weight at all. She really is such a tiny creature. I peer over the edge, but I can't even see her in the dark.

Fingernails rake my back and I scream out. I turn and thrust the spear into the chest of an infected man. It jams and the creature merely grunts as I try to pull it free. I step backwards, mindful of the cliff behind me. Six of them surround me – all muttering, all staggering in some kind of hallucinogenic state. All crying out for help.

They are like trolls. In the last dregs of daylight, their skin seems blistered and green. "Get away from me, trolls," I scream. They grumble something back in response but I don't understand. Sounds seem hazy all of a sudden.

I look around for another weapon, but all I see is a snake wrapped around my stomach. It's trying to eat me. I wrestle with it, unwrap it from my body and toss it aside. It lashes out at me, so I jump on the villainous serpent and kick it over the edge of the cliff. There's a tiny voice inside, telling me that the snake was important for some reason. The trolls moan and mutter as well.

A wash of orange and crimson lingers along the eastern horizon. The trolls are bleeding, painting the sky with blood. I turn to run but a huge dragon sits in the valley below. Eyes blaze near its massive mouth. Its tail flickers, scales shining bright orange. A ferocious creature. Nothing could tame such a wild beast. The world is becoming hazy, yet I see it so clearly. Finally, everything seems clear.

A mouse. A mouse runs towards the dragon. It scampers quickly. Go little mouse. Go. The dragon opens more eyes – dozens of eyes all scrutinising the little rodent. The dragon's mouth opens and swallows the poor creature whole.

"No." As I cry out, a voice inside tells me not to be sad. Maybe the mouse will give the dragon indigestion. Maybe the dragon will see the mouse wriggling inside its stomach and the dragon will fall from the bleeding sky.

Come on foul beast. Let's fly together. I spread my wings and jump out from the cliff. For a moment, I soar. The two dragons soar together. All dragons can fly, but eventually all dragons will fall.

Untitled

In the dark she sings,
She holds my hand tight in hers;
Limbs tender, voice soft.
Clouds part, the shines upon
Green skin, one too many arms.

Tek-tonic

Through the ship's portal, the planet loomed: a swirling mass of white clouds illuminated against the black backdrop beyond.

Sliding towards the main console, Karazu greeted Sari, who looked up with her bright valiant eyes. Her optimism filled him with hope.

"It will be okay," Sari's voice echoed within his thoughts.

"Maybe?" Karazu blocked his thoughts to everyone except Sari. The crew's courage hung tenuously by a thread; they did not need to sense his doubt. He punched a few commands in the console, bringing up the planetary statistics. "Commander, what is our proximity status," said Karazu. It was the first time he had communicated audibly since the ship entered this star system.

"We will be entering the planet's atmosphere in moments Captain." The Commander looked anxiously at Karazu.

It was an expectant look. Karazu felt as if he was meant to alleviate their fears, but he could not control his own anxieties.

"Thankyou Commander, please engage heat shields." If he kept talking aloud, it may help stop the rest of the crew from sensing his fear.

"Yes sir." The Commander returned his focus to the console.

Karazu felt the weight of their entire race upon his shoulders. He looked at the monumental size of the planet in the portal. The planet's magnitude dwarfed the ship and his hope. Their tiny ships were going to be pulverised by the heat and gravity.

"There is nothing to be worried about," Sari penetrated his thoughts. "Our ships are tiny, but the heat shields have been improved since the colonies last attempt to land on the planet."

"How do you do that?"

"You can't block your thoughts from me." Sari smiled. She quivered and siliceous membranes divided and reformed into a slender appendage. In mimicry, his gelatinous brown ovoid body formed an arm and held her hand.

Through the starboard portal, the hundreds of allied ships sailed alongside him: the last of the Siliconeous beings. Carbon was the new silicon, the new evolutionary path. If this descent failed, there would be no more chances. By now, their home galaxy would be nothing more than a pit of black holes. Planets would be boiling out of existence as ancient stars went nova. The age of sophistication would be lost along with all the discoveries of the Siliconeous race: space travel, faster than light communication, self-regeneration, telepathy and the origins of space and time itself.

"This is just a new beginning. Our race will persist." Sari interrupted his thoughts.

Karazu shrugged. "Of all the planets our ancestors explored this was the only one that was habitable. What happens if we can't land? What happens if we endure the same fate? There is no one back home to carry out a new voyage."

"When our ancestors attempted to land all those thousands of years ago, they did not know what we do about this planet. Our technology and heat shields have improved significantly since then. We should be able to land." Sari's optimism started to wane. A hint of doubt lingered in her thoughts.

Karazu looked around at the crew. Few were still seated. Most stood looking through the windows at the planet, as it grew closer. Only the Commander continued fiddling with dials and plotting trajectories. Karazu pierced the Commander's thoughts. He was terrified. The Communications Officer stood pondering their ancestors who had been lost. The last messages from the old space fleets had been horrific, recalling every detail as the ship's heat shields yielded to the thick atmosphere. The old ships had melted and fell like thousands of falling tears. When they had crashed, they cooled and had become nothing more than solidified glassy tombs scattered across their landing site.

Even the cook now stood on the bridge, watching their decent. "We are going to plummet to our doom, like our ancestors did."

Karazu tried to block out the crew's thoughts. He focused upon Sari, but this time even she did not have any comforting thoughts to console him.

"We are entering the atmosphere Captain." The Commander looked up from the console at the window. "I never imagined the planet would be so large."

Karazu remained silent. He had no thoughts that would bring hope to the crew. The fate of the crew, the fleet, the whole race was now out of his hands.

A jolt thundered through their craft followed by a hypnotic creaking. The heat was melting the external layers.

"Commander, activate heat shields to their maximum. Redirect all remaining power to the shields," Karazu said coming back to reality.

The Commander programmed the sequence instantly. The ship whirred as power was rerouted to the shields.

The ship fell into silence: a prolonged silence. Everyone's thoughts were directed on the same subject on whether the shields were going to hold. Karazu tried hopelessly to shut out the thoughts of his shipmates. Their thoughts were amplified by the silence that surrounded him.

A low drawn out mew broke the silence. Creaking. The ship was still succumbing to the pressure and heat.

Karazu shut his eyes; he did not need to see. Sari's and the rest of the crew's fear radiated through his core. Through the emptiness of space and across a distance and time too vast to measure, Karazu felt the muted cries of all he had left behind and all the space fleets who had sacrificed themselves before him. He had to give his crew hope. He had to be strong for his crew, for the fleet, for Sari. She had always held him together when he felt helpless. It was his turn to give her hope.

"This time our descent will work." Karazu beamed his thoughts boldly to all the crew and the ships sailing alongside him.

The ship started to flatten under the pressure. The Silicon bodies onboard trembled with the gravity.

"This was expected, but the inner heat shields will hold." Karazu said confidently.

He sensed the crew's optimism increase.

"We will land, colonise and make this new world our home."

From the other ships thoughts of encouragement echoed within him.

"And what happens if our heat shields do not hold?" For the first time since they set sail, Sari seemed terrified.

Karazu held her tight. He couldn't help but imagine their silicon bodies melting as the plummeted to their doom.

Sari's shuddered internally.

Karazu held Sari's hand tightly. So tight his knuckles turned yellow and started to crystallise. "Our landing will work. But if it doesn't at least we will be fused as one."

Sari broke a smile; the fear was swept away from her thoughts and replaced by the only thought that would comfort them both. "No matter what happens we will be together."

***

The tour guide released a stifled yawn. Frustrated she looked at her watch, counting the minutes before the bus came to pick them up.

She got the stragglers to regroup. A gusty Nullarbor wind skittled dust around, biting at the skin of inappropriately dressed bare-ankled tourists.

"Wow! Now this is exciting. I haven't seen one of these in years." She bent down and picked up the strategically placed black object in her hands, cradling it like a newborn child. "Does anyone know what this is?" she asked. Contrived enthusiasm oozed from every pore in her sweaty being.

A few shrugs, a couple of "I don't knows" and as usual one young boy facetiously proclaiming it was "a bleeding rock'.

"This is a tektite. They are only found in several places across the world, but most are found in Indonesia the Philippines and..." she prompted, looking at the youngsters.

"Australia" said a few vivacious juveniles in union.

"That's right. They are very old, some dating back over millions of years. These ones here are possibly over 700,000 years old." She lowered her voice to an eerie whisper. "They have a brown glassy surface inside and some scientists believe they might have come from the moon." She sensed a few ears pricking up. Right she had them now, if she could just hold their attention she would be able to get through the rest of the tour.

She rabbited on, as she always did, with her rehearsed spiel. "They have high levels of silicon like moon dirt and are unlike any other rocks on earth."

"They aren't from the moon. They are just any old earth rocks," interrupted a brutish man.

The tour guide flashed a penetrating sideways glance. She looked at her watch. Five more minutes, just five more minutes.

"Maybe it came from Mars," said an enthusiastic child.

"I doubt it, they tend to be found in large patches and would have been scattered more randomly if they came from somewhere more distant than the moon... speaking of somewhere more distant, here's our ride back to town." She relaxed as she saw the dust billowing up behind her motorised saviour.

The group poured onto the bus chatting indiscernibly as she dropped the rock down carelessly for the next tour guide.

Preoccupied with the relief of the cool climate-controlled bus, she did not notice the rock shatter in two, nor did she notice the gel like substance that slid out onto the ochre plains, she did, however, hear an insistent voice echoing inside her head.

"When we first studied this planet, it was not quite this warm. Can you turn the air-conditioning up a fraction?"

She looked around and saw nothing but empty dusty plains. Confused she shook her head "Too much heat. I must be going mad."

The Last Polar Bear

From her warm den, she emerges. Even though it was a short winter, the sun is a stranger. Above the snow-speckled slopes, an enormous bird hovers. Its loud chopping squawk is like no gull, eagle or falcon she has ever heard.

She stands guard over her den as the strange bird flies over the white plains. The snow has already started to melt. Her stomach grumbles. No time to waste. It is time to feed.

#

The helicopter veered towards the chequered pattern of roofs flanked by snow. Aiden gripped the handrail, taking deep breaths.

"Look! Polar bear." Mick propped his sunnies on top of his head and peered out of the window.

"Where?" said Aiden, letting go of the handrail.

"Down there."

Aiden looked directly below. The roofs of the town were tiny coloured squares amongst endless white smothering the ground far *far* below.

Aiden clasped his mouth. "Oww! I think I'm going be sick."

"Polar bears?" The pilot had been silent during their journey but turned his head abruptly. "Didn't think you youngsters were serious?"

"Sure. Quick expedition before uni starts," said

Mick. "We know we probably won't see one, but you never know."

"What! You mean there wasn't a polar bear down there?" Aiden growled at Mick.

"Sorry." Mick slapped him on the back. "Couldn't help it."

The pilot chuckled and took the chopper lower. Black Spruce bowed under the force as they descended upon the outskirts of town.

Aiden's boots sunk deep into the snow when he disembarked and the feeling of ground beneath his feet calmed his stomach.

"Here you are boys," said the pilot, hauling their hiking gear from the underside of the chopper and dumping it on the snow. "3D cameras, tranquilizer darts? You're optimistic."

Aiden ignored the pilot's goading tone and squinted at his surroundings. Rusty train tracks peered through the snow; signs dangled from their hinges; shops were boarded up with planks; and between two train carriages, the lake glistened with a reticent gleam.

"It's awfully quiet," he said.

"Yeah. Tourism market crashed back in the 2050s. Don't see many folk travelling this far north no more," said the pilot, scooting back into his chopper. "But best of luck to ya. Polar bears," he muttered to himself. "Oh, my." The pilot laughed and took off.

Aiden and Mick ignored the pilot's lack of optimism and set off around the lake. Aiden walked in a daydream. The extended daylight hours played havoc with his sense of time but eventually the sun lost interest in the world. The glaring white plain became a silver glow and Midas came out of hiding and turned every rock and blade of grass to gold.

As they set up the tent, Mick pulled off his gloves with his teeth and positioned the camera next to the thawing lake.

"Glad you have your priorities right."

"Too right." He blew on his hands. "I want a time lapse of the stars." He put his gloves back on and retreated to the tent. "All we need now is some scotch and a woman to keep us warm."

"Sorry, didn't pack that." Aiden smiled and shuffled down in his sleeping bag.

Five seconds later, snoring resonated through the tent. "Mick!" Aiden prodded him, but Mick just grumbled.

Aiden wriggled out of his sleeping bag and wandered outside. The night air pierced his jacket and snow tumbled against his ankles as the wind suddenly intensified. It whistled across the lake with an indiscernible melody and lashed at his jacket. Aiden retreated to the tent, but as he did so, he tripped over the camera.

"Mick's going to kill me." He picked it up and scanned the images.

Flicking back through the photos, stars sailed in a semi-arc across the viewfinder and then there was a flash of white.

"Mick!" Aiden barely heard his voice against the howling wind. He returned to the shot and focused on the image. A white appendage? He clicked on the viewfinder and rotated the 3D image to look at it from another angle. A furry torso?

"Mick!" he shouted again.

Aiden heard his name echo on the wind. He spun in the direction of the voice, saw something white in front of his face and then everything went dark.

#

When Aiden awoke, springs dug into his back and a musky smell lingered in the air. Outside, the ocean roared; maybe he was back at his gran's coastal cottage. He craned his neck. Next to the bed, unfamiliar faces stared at him from a photo on the bedside table. A thick bearded man with a semi-toothless grin sat on the deck of a boat. Alongside him, a flaxen-haired woman held a blonde blue-eyed child on her lap. Next to the photo sat a silver locket, similar to his gran's. Disorientated, he propped himself up and opened the locket; it wasn't his grandmother looking back. Instead, a few fine strands of blonde hair were looped inside. This wasn't his gran's house. The roaring of the ocean intensified. Gingerly, he wandered across to the window. He peered between planks boarding up the window and saw the wind roar. Wind not waves. Wind... snow... blizzard.

He rushed towards the door. A teenage version of the white-haired child from the photo stood in the doorway. She was rugged up in a white jacket and thick white gloves. With her platinum blonde hair, she looked like an angel.

She pointed down the hallway. Aiden followed her directions. Dusty photos in chipped ornate frames covered the walls: mountains of white, seals and countless landscapes. Beautiful photos neglected and decomposing.

The hallway opened up into a large dining room and kitchen. A fireplace crackled nearby. The scenery was homey, yet the furniture derelict.

Mick and an old man sat at a huge wooden table. Bread and cheese were laid out before them.

"You "ook "ike crap," Mick said with his mouth full.

"Ursula, find another chair," muttered the old man.

Ursula hurried back down the hallway.

The man reached across Mick and grabbed a chunk of bread from a fresh loaf. "Better get some before your friend eats this month's rations."

Ursula tapped Aiden on the shoulder and offered a chair. Her white hair shimmered in the light of the fire.

"Thank you."

She looked down shyly and stepped away from the table.

Aiden touched his swollen lip. "What happened? Where are we?"

"Dr Foreston brought us back to town in his Tundra Buggy." Mick nodded towards the old man.

"So we're safe. The polar bear isn't going to attack us here?"

Dr Foreston grunted, spraying breadcrumbs across the table. "Polar bear! Hah, not likely. Even if there were still alive, they wouldn't look at you twice unless you were a plump hundred pound seal."

"I saw one. Well... I saw something... on the camera."

"Nothing attacked us," said Mick.

"What, I just fell did I?"

"It was just a late winter blizzard. The tent pole probably hit you. It went flying when the winds hit. Ripped the tent apart," said Mick.

"But I saw something white before I fell."

"Saw something white? Out here? In the snow? Couldn't be." Mick smiled.

Aiden rolled his eyes. He looked at the old man: unkempt hair, rugged and abrupt. A stark contrast to the young and reserved Ursula. She wandered around the kitchen tinkering with dishes. She turned and for a moment, he saw glimpse of a tight-lipped smile.

"Aren't you eating?" Aiden asked.

Ursula clenched the china plate she was holding in her gloves, her eyes dancing nervously between the faces at the table.

"She can have her supper later. Now it is time to do the dishes. *Isn't it,* Ursula?"

She stared with pleading eyes and then retreated to the kitchen.

"That's a bit harsh," said Mick. "You can't keep her secluded from the rest of the world. It's so isolated out here."

"Don't tell me how to raise my daughter. I've raised her myself and she's fine."

Mick slumped in his chair and drummed his fingers on the table. "Where's her mother?"

"Boating accident," Dr Foreston kept his eyes firmly fixed on his food. "Ursula nearly drowned too."

Mick looked at Ursula. "I'm sorry."

"So what are you doing out here, Dr Foreston? Are you the local GP?" asked Aiden, changing subject.

"No." Dr Foreston glared. "I was researching arctic wildlife. Genetics and climate change adaptations, that sort of thing."

"Arctic wildlife?" piped up Mick.

"Beluga whales, polar bears and other threatened species."

"So you'd know the best place to spot polar bears?" Excitement prickled Aiden's skin.

Even Mick stopped eating.

"*Was* researching. Past tense. I haven't seen one in years."

Aiden cradled his head deep in thought. "You must've seen one. You're here all the time." He looked up when Dr Foreston didn't reply. "There were reported sightings. Sure, they might be elusive, but—"

"There are no polar bears. You made sure of that," Dr Foreston interjected.

"What! What have we done?" Mick stiffened.

"You... you're all the same. Driving your gas guzzlers, living in your square city cubes. Don't worry if you melt my home, you can always just turn up the air-conditioning back home."

Mick stood up, grating his chair on the floorboards. "Steady on."

Dr Foreston stormed out of the room. "Frequent flying fools, getting stuck out here..." He voice trailed off as he retreated down the hallway.

"Okay," began Mick. "He's clearly a raving loony."

"Keep your voice down." Aiden spotted Ursula. She stood in the kitchen, unresponsive, focused on the dishes. "Poor girl."

"Don't even think about cutting my lunch again. I saw her first," jibed Mick.

"Really!" said Aiden. "We almost died and you're trying to pick up?"

"We didn't almost die."

Mick looked at Ursula as she approached the table to collect dishes. "Do you want a hand?" Mick reached for a plate.

Ursula's hand arrived first and his hand rested on her gloved fingers. She retracted her hand and rushed down the hallway.

"She's probably your type anyway," said Mick. "You tend to attract the crazy ones."

"She's just been separated from the outside world too long," said Aiden.

"As soon as the blizzard stops, we should get back

out there. On our way here, I saw a large storage shed that might have tents. It's not like anyone's around to care." Mick put on his jacket. "I'll be back soon. Behave while I'm gone." Mick cocked an eyebrow as he left the house.

Aiden wandered down the hallway. On his right, the musty smell wafted from his room. Ursula stood by the bedside table.

"Are you okay?" he asked.

In her glove, she cradled the silver locket. Her eyes gazed to some other place or some other time.

"Is this your mother?" Aiden picked up the photo frame. "You must miss her."

Ursula's dark eyes showed no sign of loss or recollection and she simply laid the locket back on the bedside table.

Aiden waited for her to respond, until it was unbearable. "Can I use your bathroom?"

Without words, Ursula led him across the hall to a cool tiled bathroom.

The musty smell of the bedroom subsided, replaced by something pungent: a mixture reminiscent of part-hospital and part-pub. Dozens of jars cluttered the bathroom windowsill. Inside the jars, animal remains floated in clear fluid: bones, claws and pinkish bits Aiden assumed were organs. Traces of the doc's past research? Aiden turned to Ursula to ask, but she'd already disappeared.

Tiptoeing across the floor, out of fear of knocking anything over, he turned on the taps above the basin and splashed water on his face. Above him, the bathroom cabinet beckoned. Curiosity overcame him and he discovered dozens of used razors. Traces of Dr Foreston's hair clogged the blades. The old man certainly hadn't shaven recently. Puzzled, he picked up one of the razors and tugged at the fine white hairs in the blades.

A guttural scream interrupted his train of through. Aiden ran to the window and peered outside. Through the falling snow, he saw a glimpse of two polar bears. And Mick was out there with them.

Aiden raced out of the bathroom, down the corridor and out the front door. Cold stabbed him as he looked upon the deserted township. Something growled in the distance. Along the snow-covered street, creamy fur glistened in the light. Long snout, beady eyes and tubby belly — that was how he recalled polar bears. He envisaged them sliding playfully on bellies and pounding ice sheets in search of seals. Occasionally standing on hind legs, but he didn't remember them walking so upright.

"Dr Foreston," Aiden shouted towards the house. "We need help." Aiden took a cautious few steps down the street. The polar bear mimicked him, walking with surprising agility. And it kept walking. Cold and numbness penetrated Aiden's feet, moved through his legs and into his chest, which froze in an agonising spasm. This was too close for comfort. He rushed back to the house.

He tugged on the door handle. It didn't budge. "Dr Foreston! Open the door. Ursula!" The bears walked faster. They almost ran.

"Come on, open the door." He rammed it with his shoulder. The handle turned and he fell forward.

Flat on the floor, he panted with icy breath. "Polar bears, two. Huge. And quick."

"Hah! I think you hit your head too hard." Dr Foreston ignored Aiden and walked down the hallway.

"Wait! Mick needs help."

The doctor didn't respond.

Aiden rushed to the phone and called the pilot.

"You need to pick us up now," he screamed down the line when the pilot answered.

"Huh," mumbled the pilot.

Someone knocked on the wooden door. Shit, Mick was still out there.

"Just get here soon." Aiden hung up and raced to the door. He opened it and stared into black beady eyes and a white furry face.

The bear growled.

Aiden screamed.

He staggered backwards and fell near the fireplace. The bear picked up a fire poker, holding it deftly in its paws. He'd only seen polar bears in old documentaries, but he was sure their paws weren't so slender.

He scanned the fireplace for another weapon: an iron pipe, a stick, anything. As the bear loomed down, Aiden grabbed a handful of ash and hurled it at the bear's face.

It howled and pawed at its eyes.

He dodged the beast and ran down the hallway. "Dr Foreston! Ursula!"

He flung each door open along the corridor, only to be greeted by vacant musty rooms.

He flung open the last door along the corridor and tumbled down a small flight of stairs, hitting his head as he landed. The pungent smell in the room stood out more than the throbbing in his head. Aiden finally recognised the hospital-pub like smell from the bathroom: formaldehyde, which he and Mick used in biology classes. He rubbed his head and gazed around the laboratory.

In the dim light, he spotted benches with Bunsen burners, vials and more specimen jars. Beakers connected to tubes and cylinders spanned the extent of the benches. Aiden's skin tingled.

A dull wooden thud resonated above him. Aiden looked up and saw another staircase leading to an open trapdoor, swinging in the breeze. Something dripped down from the trapdoor onto the floorboards. He touched the sticky liquid. Red liquid. The trail of blood led down the stairs and towards a bench in the far corner of the room. The bench was dotted body parts, vials of blood. And a severed foot with a snow-boot still attached.

Mick?

Aiden's hold on reality began to fray at the edges. Dry-retching, he stumbled backwards into a bench. A cylinder toppled and shattered like crystal confetti on the floor. From the glass wreckage, a foetal being stirred sluggishly before collapsing.

Guttural howling resonated from the doorway as a polar bear descended the stairs. Aiden raced for the trapdoor and careered into Dr Foreston.

"What have you done? I think the bears have killed Mick!" A lump grew in his throat, a mixture of anger and grief. "We need to find Ursula. We need to leave. Your crazy breeding program has gone wrong."

"Hah. Polar bears!" Dr Foreston's arms were suddenly around Aiden neck pressing on his windpipe. "What is the point of breeding more polar bears if they can't adapt? But if they had *our* dexterity combined with *their* strength, they would be invincible. If they are to survive they need to be more brutal, more aggressive, more... human."

"What!" gasped Aiden, tugging at Dr Foreston's

arms.

"Do you know how long it takes to get rations of meat here?"

The polar bear growled and staggered forward on hind legs.

Aiden's chest tightened. "You fed... Mick to... them?"

"Don't be absurd. Not all of him."

The creature raised its slender paws above Aiden's head. Aiden scanned the bench for any sign of a weapon. No jars sat in close range, just Mick's foot. He let go of Dr Foreston's grip around his neck and grasped at the bloody foot.

"Hah! A foot is no use against a thousand pounds of muscular flesh. However, it is very useful for DNA. My babies don't breed. I need fresh DNA specimens. You on the other hand..."

As the creature's claw descended, Aiden rammed the foot into Dr Foreston's groin. Yelping, the doc clutched his groin and released his grip.

Aiden ran for the trapdoor and the bear swiped at Dr Foreston's head instead. The doctor fell to the floor with his neck bent at an acute angle. The creature looked up from the doctor's limp body and growled. Aiden raced through the trapdoor, out onto snow.

As he ran from the scene, his tears solidified in frozen rivulets. He stopped to rest against a giant tundra buggy with mammoth tyres towering over his head. Growling resonated down the road. He hid inside the buggy and had a moment of relief until the handle of the tundra buggy turned. A polar bear stepped inside and walked down the aisle with methodical steps. Aiden raced to the back of the buggy and jimmied open a window. His stomach churned at the long *long* drop below. He shut his eyes, took a breath and jumped.

Aiden's knees crumpled beneath him as he landed in a patch of pink snow. He inspected his limbs for wounds and then realised the blood wasn't his. He looked up and saw Ursula crouched over a lifeless Mick. Her head hung low and white hair flowed across her face concealing her distress. Mick's jacket was shredded, the insulated lining ripped out. Gashes chequered his torso and face. Aiden let out a whimper and placed his hand on Ursula's shoulder.

"It's too late for Mick. The polar bears aren't polar bears. Your dad's mad." He wiped the tears from his cheek and squatted beside her. Ursula's white gloves lay upon Mick's motionless chest. Aiden picked them up.

"Here. We need to go now." Aiden said consolingly and handed her the gloves.

Ursula's hands clasped the gloves, her paws clasped the gloves, her white furry paws clasped the gloves.

Aiden recoiled.

Ursula peered up at him with a mixed look of confusion and empathy. Her mouth was covered in blood. She stared at Aiden helplessly with dark eyes.

"Wha... who..." Aiden staggered backwards. "But... you're human, you're..."

Ursula wiped her mouth with the back of her slender paw, smearing blood across her face. Now pink, he could see her face was covered in a fine white down. They weren't Dr Foreston's razors.

"The lock of hair — you didn't survive. Ursula didn't survive, did she?"

She seemed to search for some distant memory. The words "Ursula" formed on her slender lips without sound.

"He couldn't save you and your mother, but he had your lock of baby hair. He could bring you back. He could give you strength and swimming ability, enough to survive another tragedy." A cold shiver rippled over Aiden's skin. Growling intensified behind him, but he stood frozen. He should be scared, but she didn't look like the others; she still looked human. "We need to go. It's okay, we'll get you help."

Ursula's mouth parted revealing yellowing blood stained teeth and she growled.

Aiden dropped the gloves and fled. He raced down the side streets and alleyways. His feet sank deep into the snow as if he was running through quicksand. Heading for the lake, he ran out onto the ice until there was nothing but dark blue water in front of him.

The lake crooned softly as a light wind wafted onto the land. Behind him, something growled; below him, something creaked. He looked around. A creature wandered from town towards the lake, another approached from the right of the lake and two staggered on their hind legs to his left. Aiden took a step backwards. The ice cracked. He hit water; icy water hit him back, like knives piercing his skin.

Gasping, he breached the surface only to see four white creatures on the shore. A paw swung. He ducked under the water and bobbed up again several feet away. Icy water crept down his jacket collar and down his back, burning his skin. With heavy water-laden clothes, he kept swimming until the creatures were dots on the horizon.

He veered out at a right angle, hoping to hit the shore again. Crystal blue surrounded him: an expansive liquid desert. He looked around. Nothing. Nothing but water.

Fatigued and wheezing, he stopped. His legs and arms felt like lead weights. Aiden's head ducked under the water. A rush of cold seared his brain. He thrashed his arms bringing himself back to the surface and tried to swim further.

He swam endlessly. The blue engulfed him. Above, around and below — nothing but chilly blue. No white. No ice. Nothing solid.

His head ducked under the water and he gasped. Liquid silence.

Then an angelic chopping noise resonated from the skies. In a last ditch attempt, Aiden thrashed at the water to stay afloat. A ladder fell from a helicopter above. With every ounce of strength that remained, he grasped the ladder and pulled himself up into the helicopter.

He lay panting next to the pilot. "G-g-go now," he said shivering.

The pilot looked around at the white furry creatures surrounding the lake. "Polar bears. Wow. They don't look quite like I imagined."

"Yes, they're slightly different." Aiden sat up and peered out the window.

The pilot hovered above the snow plains. "Wait, there's someone down there... a young lady. Geez, polar bears and girls. You boys did alright."

Aiden spotted Ursula, her face stained with blood.

"She looks injured. We have to help her. The polar bears might hurt her," said the pilot.

Aiden lifted the helicopter pilot's earmuffs and screamed hoarsely, "There are no more polar bears. Go!"

#

From the hillside, she sees the lake has completely thawed. She sniffs the air and walks down the hill away from her den. A ball of fur follows her. And another. The cubs flop onto their bellies and glide down the snowy slope. They toss and turn over one another playfully. As her cubs suckle up to her, she gazes upwards. High in the sky the strange eagle soars, hastily flying south for spring.

Bloodletting

"Pulse tacky. Arterial bleed."

"Spinal board."

Words. Many words. Many voices.

"Fractured patella."

Words and distant screaming. And sobbing.

I try to catch their meaning. Lights distract. Wailing. Confusion. Movement. Click clack of a trolley. Ceiling lights flash above me and fade.

#

An intravenous pole towers by my side. Drips of clear fluid glide hypnotically down the line towards my left arm. Someone's removed my friendship band and silver bangle that Mum bought for my twenty first birthday and shackled my wrist with a green plastic identification band. As consciousness returns so does the pain. A searing stabbing sensation in my right knee.

"Nurse!" I find my voice, though it is hoarse. I try to crane my neck to find the buzzer, but a brace stops me. I remember someone saying spinal board. A pang of fear ripples across my skin. I focus on my toes and they obediently wiggle. Relief fills me. The brace and board must've just been a precaution, but the pain in my knee is real.

"Nurse!" I cast my eyes left and right. The room is vacant, except for a pale-skinned girl with flaming red hair. She stands in the doorway. Her white hospital gown flutters although I feel no breeze.

"Hello." I lift my hand from the bed and wave.

The girl mimics me. Her lips peel upwards into a tight-lipped smile, but the movement is unnatural as if she finds the action unfamiliar.

"How old are you?"

She holds up three fingers, inspects them, then adds another.

"Four?"

She nods and takes a step into my room.

"Are you a patient?" She certainly doesn't look well: eyes glazed and red, skin sickly yellow and anaemic.

She shakes her head.

"You have a hospital gown on. You should probably be in bed. Why are the nurses letting you roam about?"

She shrugs.

"Well, can you find my buzzer?"

She cocks her head to one side and the smile vanishes. As she steps closer, the lights dim. The green light from the blood pressure monitor gleams on her face, making her look sicklier. Ghostly even. She bends down by my bed and picks up the buzzer.

"Can you press it? My knee is killing me."

She glances at the blanket covering my legs and pulls it back. Blood soaked bandages cover my legs. The sight accentuates the pain.

"Please." I reach out for the buzzer.

She looks at the device in her pale hands and squeezes. It crumbles in her tiny palm. Plastic dust sprinkles through her fingers as if she's playing in a sandpit.

Perhaps it is just the dim light, but her eyes seem to darken til it's hard to tell pupil from iris.

I must be dreaming or unconscious. She opens her mouth as if to speak, but instead pokes a black tongue at me, though it barely resembles a tongue. It is almost leech-like, wiggling and pulsating.

She crawls onto my bed and clutches her stomach.

"You aren't real. You aren't real." I pinch my leg and it hurts. "I must be feverish." I touch my forehead, but my hand only feels damp gauze. Running my fingers through my long hair, they feel sticky. I inspect my palm. The sight of blood makes my stomach curdle.

Her eyes turn to my hand and they widen with delight.

She lets go of her stomach, revealing a growing ring of blood-soaked linen.

"Oh, God. You're bleeding. Nurse," my voice croaks.

The girl's skin turns whiter. She crawls closer and straddles my right arm, pinning my hand to the bed.

"What are you doing? Nurse!"

Her tongue drools and droops lower like a wriggling snake til it latches onto the crevice of my arm. The veins in my upper arm pulsate. Blue ridges rise under the surface of my skin. The tongue pulsates. Tiny bulges travel along it as she siphons my blood, my life.

The room spins. Shivers prickle my skin. Suddenly I'm cold.

"Nurse!" I push the girl with my other arm, but she does not budge. I rip the neck-brace off so I can move. A bedpan sits next to the bed. With my left arm, I swing it hard whacking her on the side of the head. She falls, releasing her leech-like grip, and the bedpan clanks on the linoleum floor.

Footsteps echo outside. The girl stands, regains her composure and her eyes lose their intense darkness.

"What's going on in there?" A female voice asks nearby.

She turns to the door and runs. The lights shine brighter as she flees.

A nurse enters moments later. Her eyes widen.

"Did you see her?" I ask.

She ignores my question and rushes to my bed. "It's only precautionary, but you can't take this off." She picks up the neck brace. "Despite everything that happened, we are here to help you."

"What happ..." The room blazes white. My head is so light it feels as if it is floating. "I feel dizzy. The girl..."

"Don't worry about the mother and daughter right now."

Mother? Daughter? Something lingers in the back of my mind. I try to grab onto that thought buried beneath the layers of confusion and drowsiness.

"No wonder you're dizzy. Your BP's dropped." She inspects my left arm, lifting it up as if I'm a ragdoll. "And you've ripped your needle out when you had your little tantrum."

"Tantrum? It was the girl ... the injured girl with the weird tongue." I realise how ridiculous it sounds. I try to sit up, but the world objects; everything dances. My knee burns. "Pain," I manage to mutter.

"I'll be back with the doctor and we'll see if we can work out what's going on with your blood pressure." She strolls away from me, picking up the bedpan on the way to the door. "I have other patients to tend to." She flashes me a sideways glace before leaving. "Those who deserve treatment," she mutters just loud enough for me to hear.

What? My head pounds with confusion. Did I do something to upset her? I clasp my temples and try to focus on what happened, but there is just blackness and the chilling words: arterial bleed.

A doctor enters. Her white lab coat dances across the floor. She is speaking and taking blood but everything seems to blur. And I'm so confused and tired. They are here. I can drift off for a second and still be safe, I tell myself as I let my eyes close.

#

It feels as if seconds have passed, but when I wake the nurse is standing by my bed holding my wrist with two fingers and the doctor alongside her.

"Your haemoglobin dropped so we gave you a blood transfusion." The doctor sits on the side of my bed.

I inspect the bag of dark fluid on the pole beside me. It's already half empty so who knows how long I slept.

"We don't know why it dropped so low," she continues. "There's no sign of internal bleeding and your scratches shouldn't have caused *that* much blood loss. But we're doing some more blood tests."

"Scratches?"

"Yes, you hit your head and smashed up your knee in the accident and had a mild concussion but it's nothing to worry about. Just try to rest."

"Accident?" Images pop into my head of blue and red flashing lights dazzling on the shattered car windscreen. And there were words. "Arterial bleed." The words escape me before I have a chance to comprehend their meaning. "Is that why?"

"Your arteries are fine." The doctor draws up fluid in a syringe. "I think you should get some rest. You're still suffering some side-effects of the concussion." She injects the fluid into the needle.

"What's that?"

"You were complaining before of pain. It might make you a bit drowsy, but this will give you some relief."

"No! I can't sleep. The girl ... the creature. I didn't imagine it. I couldn't have. It was real." Or maybe it wasn't. Maybe it was just the concussion.

She smiles patronisingly, as if I'm insane, and strides from the room. Just like that, she leaves me alone with the nurse who hasn't smiled or reassured me once.

The nurse drops my wrist back down. "Your pulse is fine and BP's stable again, I'll be back in fifteen to check again." Her voice is curt; her mannerisms lack any kind of manners.

The pain in my knee begins to ease and the drowsiness sets in til my eyelids are too heavy to keep open.

#

A tugging sensation drives me from my slumber. The girl's ravenous tongue sucks at the nook of my arm. I rip my arm from her grasp. She seems content to let me go and sits cross-legged at the end of my bed with her hands folded neatly in her lap.

"What do you want from me?"

She cocks her head towards the intravenous line. The bag is half-full. Is she waiting for it to fill into me so she can just take more? Her black eyes hold me in a piercing glare. For a moment, her skin colour almost looked normal, but as she sits and stares, the peaky yellow starts to show, as if the blood won't stop draining from her body.

"I've never hurt you. Why are you punishing me?"

She cocks her head.

Tears well in my eyes. I don't have the strength to call out and can't bear to hear the nurse condemn me as insane. "Why me?"

Her intense stare pierces my soul. She looks at me as if I know why she is here. Her eyes turn to the blood transfusion bag again. Tiny hands grasp my wrist.

I try to wriggle it free, but her long leech tongue drains my veins, making me weaker by the second. The dizziness returns and the cold. Life extracted. Body failing. By my side there is beeping. The pressure on my wrist ceases and the girl scrambles under the bed. Bright lights and beeping.

Footsteps. Are more coming to get me?

"There's nothing left to take."

"Nothing?" I can hear the nurse. For once, her cranky voice reassures me. "Just relax." I can feel her checking my needle.

More footsteps clomp on the linoleum floor.

"Her blood pressure just dropped. I don't know what happened. She was fine."

Lights shine in my eyes. I focus and make out the doctor flashing a tiny torch at me. She rubs my hand. "There must be internal bleeding somewhere. We're going to take you into surgery and find out what's going on, okay?"

I don't know if it's a question, but I don't have the energy to form a response.

Before I can make sense of everything, the bed is moving. I look back to see the girl, but she isn't there. A policeman stands outside. Is some catastrophe unfolding? Maybe the hospital is under attack by alien girls with horrid leech tentacle-like tongues. My thoughts make no sense.

The policeman looks at me.

"Your questions will have to wait," the nurse tells him.

Questions? What could he possibly want with me? I'm the one with questions, but I can't ask as the bed starts moving. We pass open curtains opposite the nurses" station. People stand around a bed sobbing. Machines beep. Through the mass of weeping bodies, I spot a young face. A girl, flame red hair plaited in pigtails, ghostly pale cheeks, face mangled, bruised, cut, body motionless. Doctors pull a sheet over her. Alongside him, a mother clasps her hand, unwilling to let go. Her arm in a sling, and even though her face is bruised she looks familiar.

Arterial bleed. I remember those words. But I just have cuts and broken knee. That's what the doctor said. A stabbing pain erupts in the back of my head.

I remember her. I remember the girl. She flew into my windscreen. I was driving home. From the pub. A lump forms in my throat. I turn back to the girl, but the bed is moving again, clanking along the floor, racing through swinging doors.

The lump in my throat seems to take over all else. My lungs betray me. I gasp for air, helpless.

"It's okay." A man dressed in gloves and gown places an oxygen mask over my mouth. "Take deep slow breaths. No need to panic."

No need to panic. How can he say that when I killed her? The man pats my hand and turns from me to chat to another lady dressed in the same attire. As they avert their gaze, a tiny hand clings to the railing on the side of the bed. The ghostly girl crawls out from underneath the bed and stands by my side. She takes no notice of the others in the room and she doesn't pin me down. Instead, she just stares at me with those black eyes.

"No amount of blood can bring you back," I whisper to her.

Clanking of metal interrupts the moment. I turn to see a trolley wheeled in.

"Sorry, what did you say?" asks a female anaesthetist.

I shake my head. I turn back to the girl, but she has vanished.

"We're going to give you some gas now. Everything will be fine," she continues.

How can it be fine?

"Are you still there," I whisper to the girl.

"We're here," the gloved man answers instead. "Nothing to fear. Can you count back from ten for us?"

I manage a nod. "Ten... nine...eight."

A tiny yellow finger pops up at the side of the bed and disappears again.

I let my arm dangle down beside the bed and the girl, ghost, personification of death, or whatever she is, latches on.

"Seven...six...five..."

She is as ravenous as ever.

Dizziness and fatigue quickly consume me, along with fear. I want to remove my hand. I want to fight for life.

"Four..." That is how old she said she was, or used to be. So many years ahead of her that I snatched way.

"Three..." My words begin to slur. The room is ablaze with white light. I relax my hand and let the ghostly girl take my guilt, knowing I will never make it to one.

Painting the sky

Arlo peered out the round portal. A final few brush stroke and his canvas would be complete. He mixed paint to form a rich orange. Winged creatures flew above his meticulously painted ocean; and amid this, he painted a blaring sun kissing the water.

"I asked you to paint the sky," said the ship's doctor. "What is this?"

"The rest of the crew has myopia. Can't you see it?" Arlo clutched his brush.

"This is space sickness. There's never been anything outside besides stars and the darkness." The doctor shook his head. "We'll keep trying. Until you accept the black."

Attrition of the soul

Nowadays, immortality costs a mere thousand terabytes of storage on the Circuit.

Words to that effect scrolled across the screen behind the receptionist's desk. Lathum tried to ignore the picturesque scenery in the background: a dashing meadow dotted with poppies and snow-capped mountains. He could explore them all, according to the marketing jargon plastered across the images.

"Got a young one coming to see you," the receptionist said over the phone.

Young? It was an interesting observation. Lathum guessed late forties appeared young around here, but he felt old.

The receptionist placed a few sheets of paper on the counter.

"You don't need to sign now, but this is the contract."

Sun beamed through the window, warming Lathum's face. He remembered one spring day, long ago, sitting on the patio with Marika.

"Sir?" The receptionist looked up at him.

"Sorry."

"The paperwork. Would you like to read it?"

"Paperwork?"

"Yes, the contract." She smiled and tapped the sheets of paper on the counter.

"Right." Lathum slapped his palm to his forehead. He studied the contract. Words. So many words. They danced on the page. He squinted, trying to focus. It was like a sheep dog trying to round up stray ewes. Every time he managed to read a sentence, he lost his train of thought on what he had read earlier. The legal jargon didn't help. "I can't..."

The receptionist acknowledged with a nod. "It's okay." You can get someone to go through it with you later. Take a seat. Mr. Wu will be with you shortly."

Lathum perched himself on the suede seats. This place was significantly more luxurious than his apartment back home. Ever since his diagnosis he'd saved and scavenged and sacrificed extravagances to afford upload.

"Greetings, Lathum." Mr. Wu entered from a side door. He was a curious man: formal tone to his voice, vinyl waistcoat with mismatching chequered pants, and thick-rimmed glasses. His clothes and mannerisms were of another era. "Please, this way if you don't mind."

Lathum followed Mr. Wu down a narrow walkway. Gleaming white walls shone from either side and up ahead they veered right as the corridor split into a y-junction. Doors were recessed into the white walls with sequential numbers painted on each door.

"Offices?" Lathum asked.

"Oh, no. Most of our work is done by computers, except for a few menial housekeeping tasks. There is no room for human error in this business."

"So, what's inside?" Lathum pointed to the door.

Mr. Wu continued for a while and stopped at door sixty-five, where a man wearing a white jumpsuit stood guard.

Mr. Wu looked into a retinal scanner and the door slid open.

"Why this room? Are this year's patients all in this room?" Lathum followed him into room. All was dark except for blue lights twinkling in the distance.

"Heavens no! Not enough room for a month's worth of clients. It's a mere coincidence. It's just I know this one is clean." There was an edge to Mr. Wu's voice. "I'm sure that's not the kind of question you really want to ask. Lights."

The room illuminated at his command. Several caskets stood in a ring around a giant computer. The clear chambers each held a person. There was even a child inside one. Its tiny body curled up in fluid like it were snug in the womb.

"Obviously, storage for potential future download costs extra, but in cases such as yours, you may wish to upload to the Circuit to save what's left of your cognitive function. When medicine advances, your body will be ready for your return."

Lathum walked up to the child's casket and peered at the panel next to it. She'd been in here for seven years. She must've been one of the first.

"They haven't found a cure for her cancer yet," said Mr. Wu. "But your situation is different. Even so, millions of people chose to live immortal lives just on the Circuit. There's never a dull moment."

"I'm sorry." Lathum pulled his Dictaphone from his breast pocket. "Do you mind? I probably won't remember our discussion later. I store lots in here. Addresses, important conversations, just in case I forget."

Mr. Wu shook his head. "Not at all. We've had dementia patients before."

Lathum switched it on and returned it to his pocket.

"And that's the best thing about the Circuit," Mr. Wu continued. "Once downloaded, we can preserve your memory. We can remind you of everything you need to know. We can halt the deterioration."

They could stop him forgetting Marika. That is all he'd ever wanted, but the thought of returning when they'd discovered a cure for dementia had its appeal. "How long will the bodies last in here?" he asked, walking up to the next body.

"As long as you need, but unlike download, storage isn't cheap."

"I've had to cut back a few luxuries," said Lathum. "But I've saved up a lot with an immortality fund."

"It's worth it."

"Why aren't you on the Circuit then?" Lathum hadn't thought about that before. If it were so good, why was this guy not indulging in immortality?

Mr. Wu chuckled. "Been there, my friend. Body and mind turned 148 last week. I was one of the first. They found a cure for my lymphoma and I had my mind uploaded again. I also download as a backup every year. Just in case the unexpected happens."

Lathum thought of Marika. Sure, there was no way they could afford uploading every single year, but if he'd known, he would have found a way. He could have preserved her mind forever. Her beautiful mind. So caring and loving.

"Are you looking to purchase download of the mind and body storage?"

Lathum shook away the guilt over Marika. He couldn't bring her back from the accident, but at least he could remember her. "Yes. Will my brain really fit with under a hundred terabytes of storage?"

"Yes. We have one of the largest download capacities at our facility. And the largest for cryo storage as well."

It seemed bizarre that his brain, everything that made him "Lathum" on the inside, would need no more storage than the latest computer game he'd been playing. There had to be more to it than electronic impulses and bits and bytes.

"We have a one hundred percent satisfaction rate, the cheapest upload and download prices in town, and about a quarter of those downloaded request cryo storage making us the largest in the country."

Mr Wu was giving him the pre-prepared promotional spiel.

"So the rest of the chambers are along this corridor?"

asked Lathum.

"And some more out the back. It takes a lot of room and energy consumption, hence the cost."

It all seemed so simple. Too simple. He'd halt the disease just like that. He'd remember Marika forever.

"Do you have family on the Circuit? You can interact with them."

"No. My ummm..." Lathum felt the brain fog drifting in like thick clouds. "My wife... Marika died suddenly."

"Sorry."

"So you just download everything?" Lathum had researched the process and knew the answer, but he wanted to change topic to avoid the whole pity party about his wife.

"Yes, just like backing up your hard-drive. We guarantee no corruption or loss of data."

Data? Had his life just been an accumulation of data?

"Your digital self can still learn and develop on the Circuit. And there are a range of avatar options, but most like to keep their basic physical appearance with a few minor modifications as they indulge." Mr. Wu laughed. Had he said something funny? Lathum struggled to concentrate.

"So where are the rest of the chambers?"

Mr Wu's eyes widened. "Like I said before, along this corridor and out the back."

Had Lathum already asked that? He'd left it too long. The signs were becoming more and more pronounced.

Mr. Wu smiled. "Would you like to see the computers?"

"No, I've seen enough. I've left this disease too long."

"Great. Let's get the receptionist to book a date for download."

A white-suited bald man ran through the door and whispered in Mr Wu's ear.

"Well, I should get to my next client," said Mr. Wu. The stress in his voice inadvertently escaped. It was an obvious lie.

"Personnel problem," he said. "Don't worry, the computer and systems here are faultless. Do you need help getting back to reception?"

Lathum shook his head. "Remind me which way to go."

"Turn right when you get outside the room, walk down the white corridor and turn left at the y-junction."

Right and left. Right and left. Lathum repeated it. *Stick in there, directions*. They all strolled from the room, although the white-suited man shuffled with haste.

"We're heading the other way but I can guide—" began Mr. Wu.

The white-suited man tapped him on the shoulder and raised an eyebrow.

Was there some kind of emergency?

"Sorry, we have to go." Mr. Wu nodded to the white suited man and they strode off. Rather hurriedly, Lathum thought.

It should've concerned him, but walking back past all the numbered doors and the millions who were stored here, he knew they were secure. No one had ever complained from this facility. There had been no reports of malfunctioning cryo or issues with upload. Most importantly, he couldn't forget Marika. His memories would be safe in the Circuit.

Lathum reached the y-junction. He should've kept repeating the instructions rather than daydreaming. He wracked his brain. He knew Mr. Wu had mentioned which way to go. The white walls looked identical. Down each path was a narrow white corridor like the one he'd come from. His brain became an aching jigsaw puzzle. None of the pieces joined.

"Start with the corners," he told himself. He observed the caskets. Mr. Wu, despite his assurances, looked concerned and then he said...

Go right and then left.

Lathum was so excited he remembered that he yelled it. The white walls didn't give him much accolade for the achievement, not even an echo. In fact, they seemed to suck his words from him. He veered right.

After a minute walking, Lathum had a feeling he'd taken the wrong turn. Had he walked this far originally? Maybe. He often lost track of time. A passageway opened up on the left. Right and left. Those were the instructions. He turned into a narrow grey walkway. Dingy and dark. It definitely didn't feel familiar.

"No family left?" Lathum heard a voice from the end of the hallway.

"No, this one's all good to go," said someone else.

The voices grew louder. It must be people in reception. He walked faster, hoping to flee the leering corridors.

"I'll reconfigure his download file so he doesn't remember," said the first voice, "and we'll make some room."

At the end of the corridor, Lathum stumbled upon an open door to his left. He smelled the smoke before he saw anything. Rancid, it hit the back of his throat making him gag loudly.

"Hey!"

Lathum looked up through smoke to see two bald men, their white jumpsuits dotted with ash. Gas masks covered their faces, but he could see eyes glaring at him.

"Who left the door open?" One of the men approached. "What are you doing here?"

Confused, Lathum stuttered. "I don't remember. I was going...somewhere."

The smoke settled, revealing a kiln. Bare feet dangled out the end. One of the men prodded them with a metal spade. It took Lathum's frazzled brain a moment to grapple with image.

"You're burning bodies!" Lavish and gleaming on the exterior, but the truth of their cost cutting measures hit him. Just as it dawned on him, something else hit him across the side of the head. He fell to his knees and someone wrenched his arms behind his back.

"Get up!"

Lathum's knees struggled to obey the command, but he was forcibly lifted to his feet and pushed further into the room. Besides the kiln, there was a large computer and a metal table in the middle of the room with shackles on the sides. Worse than that, in his peripheral vision, there was a pile of bodies. Taken from storage to make room, thawed, all evidence discarded. He tried not to look at that corner of the room as he was thrust forward, but he couldn't help it. He balked at the sight, balked at the realisation. He was convinced downloading to the Circuit was the right thing to preserve his memory of Marika, but they could do anything to a computer file. And his brain would be just that: a file to be deleted and reconfigured.

"Look, I'm lost. I didn't mean to stumble upon—"

A white suited man grabbed his legs and picked him up. They hurled him onto the metal table and pinned his arms and legs down against the cold steel.

"Wait. I just want to get back to reception."

"Download and we'll delete the last ten minutes," the men spoke to each other.

One of them typed at the computer. Once downloaded, they could alter anything.

"There's no need. I have dementia anyway! I won't remember." Lathum screamed at them. "I am Lathum. My wife was Marika." Fear brewed inside. They might take more than minutes, like his disease they could take all until he would forget himself. "Please! Listen to me! I won't tell anyone."

A man attached small electrodes to his head. His head tingled as they hit keys on the adjacent computer. Thoughts. Memories. Feelings. Lathum struggled to hold on to something. Anything. "I am Lathum. My wife..."

The men in white began to blur.

"I am Lathum. I am... I am real."

White blobs dashed back and forth. They multiplied and merged until all that remained was blinding white. It contracted to a dazzling white dot.

The dot grew again, larger and larger until it surrounded him. He stood in a white room without walls or a floor or ceiling. It was just white. A man dressed in an equally dazzling white suit with frizzy white hair materialised and floated towards him.

"Welcome to the Circuit," he spoke in an ethereal wispy voice. "We can download any places, games, activities, whatever you want. Your simulated mind can do anything."

The scenery around them changed to the snow peaked mountains of the promotional display above the receptionist's desk. He remembered. He glanced at his body. He knew it wasn't there. His mind was, but nothing felt natural. He felt no sunshine beaming on his face.

The wispy white man touched an earpiece with his finger. "Just maintenance. Okay." The scenery vanished. The whiteness took over. "Sorry, misunderstanding," he addressed Lathum, the airiness to his voice vanishing as quickly as the scenery. "Don't worry. You won't remember any of this."

Lathum swung a fist at the figure, but it passed through him and then he vanished, leaving the blazing white. Its brightness subsided and the white began to contract to a single point and then nothing.

#

Gleaming white. Lathum stood alone at the end of a narrow corridor of white. There was something familiar about the bright white. Something he thought he should remember. He scratched his head. It was in there somewhere. Stupid dementia.

He glanced up and saw a luminescent neon exit sign. Of course, he remembered now. He was here talking with Mr. Wu and on his way out. How could he forget that?

The door in front of him opened and the receptionist stood with a perfectly pleated smile. "Back again?" she asked. "Did you get all the information you needed?" The receptionist pointed an inviting hand towards the counter.

"I think so. It's a bit fuzzy and a lot to take in."

"Ready to sign the contract? Ready for immortality?" The excitement in her voice didn't appear fake. She radiated genuine honesty this time. There was authenticity there and the ancient Mr. Wu had been sincere. He could stop the disease progressing. It was all possible.

Lathum walked up to the counter, where a wad of paperwork sat.

"I know you may struggle to remember some things, but the main things we need are your personal and bank account details."

Lathum picked up the pen and twirled it in his fingers. At the top of the contract, more promotional material cluttered the page.

Over a billion people uploaded. Join the Circuit. Interact. Learn. Stay forever young.

He wrote his name at the top. At least he remembered enough to fill out that part of the form. He was Lathum. He didn't care about staying young. He just wanted to retain his cognitive function. He just wanted to remember his lost wife. Remember her cascading hair. Remember simple things like sitting in the sunshine with her on the patio in spring, feeling the warmth on his face. He'd miss that feeling. He put down the pen.

"Having trouble remembering your address?" asked the receptionist. "Like I said if you need to get someone in to help you—"

"No. I changed my mind. Sorry, I do that a lot. I just don't think this is for me."

"Really?" Her voice filled with shock. "Won't your condition worsen?"

"Yes. Natural attrition. Slow destruction until there is nothing of this mortal soul."

She gazed up at him with wide, confused eyes.

"Maybe I just need more time to think about it," he said.

She nodded with a wry smile, completely different to her fake smiles before. She didn't understand, and to be honest he wasn't sure he did either. Something just didn't feel right.

He wandered out onto the street, stepping out into the sunshine. It felt marvellous, but what was more important: the real sun beaming on his face, or remembering Marika? He darted back inside to the counter.

"Can I take these?" He picked up the contract.

"Of course."

"I need to remember Marika. I'll fill it out at home where I can look up all my details."

"Sure." The stiffly creased smile returned to her face. "If you like, I can book you in for the download next Thursday."

"Yes." He felt confident now. "Yes, that would be great. I'll get this signed and sent." He held up the contract and then walked out. If nothing else, he would remember his wife and her beauty.

As he walked to the sidewalk, a taxi cab driver leaned out the window. "Need a lift?"

Lathum looked up and down the street. "Yes. I think so."

"Where to?"

Lathum felt the pressure seizing his head. He'd definitely made the right choice. His fuzzy brain was even struggling to remember his address. "It's Connell or O'Donnel street, avenue... parade. I think it's parade."

"Let's start with a suburb," said the driver, poorly trying to conceal a smirk.

Lathum slapped his head furiously. "Wait a second. I keep my address recorded on my Dictaphone." He pulled it out of his pocked. The green light sparkled at him. "Must've forgotten to turn it off," he said. "Let me replay it, my address will be here somewhere."

###

Traditions

"Throw another shrimp on the barbeque, Cadet," the Captain yelled at Shylea over the high-pitched screams.

"They aren't shrimp. Technically..." Shylea hesitated, "shrimp have more legs than these—"

"These..." The Captain reached into the cage and grabbed one of the captured creatures around its tiny neck. Two little legs squirmed, appendages grasped futilely at the Captain's hands. "They're pinkish. They have a shell ... look like shrimp to me."

They were more than just appendages; they were arms; they had hands. Dexterous hands that clenched as if pleading for their life. It made her stomach churn.

A couple of the other soldiers laughed, some nervously, some as jovial as the Captain.

Shylea glanced at Breanne. The Lieutenant gritted her teeth and nodded. Shylea always felt as if Breanne could read her thoughts. It was as if everything they did was in sync.

"I said, put a shrimp of the barbeque," screamed the Captain again. "Are you disobeying an order, Cadet?" He walked up to Shylea and thrust his rifle in her face so close she could smell the charred metal.

Shylea glanced at the other soldiers. No one spoke. No one stepped forward. They just stood in their once camouflaged spacesuits, now stained with blood, soot and shame. She stared down the barrel, head held high. "They aren't shrimp, Captain," her voice quivered.

He lowered the gun and started laughing again. "Come on, get into the spirit of things."

"We don't actually know if it's Christmas," Breanne interrupted. "What with time dilation—"

"They're singing Christmas carols. Can't you hear them?" The Captain lowered his rifle and placed his ear close to the flaming drum he kept insisting was a barbeque. The tiny creature, still in his grasp, squirmed as the flames neared.

"We should look at the bite on your leg," interrupted Breanne. "Your veins are very ... green. Maybe we could—"

"Shush!" The Captain held a finger to his lips. "Silent night. My favourite."

The screaming was anything but silent. Shylea clasped her hands over her ears trying to block out the creatures" wailing as they scurried about in the cage looking for a way out. She glanced down. Amid the frenzied panic, one stood clasping the cage's bars, looking up at the creature in the Captain's hands.

"What are you looking at, Cadet?" The Captain strode up to Shylea and glared at her. "It might be a new world, but tradition is still important," he said. "At Christmas we always used to cook barbequed shrimp."

"I really think you should sit down, Captain." Shylea rested her hand on his shoulder. Her other hand reached out and grasped his wrist. "Why don't you let me put the shrimp on the barbeque then?"

"Don't overcook it!" He let it go and wandered away from the rest of the soldiers with a slight stagger.

Bulging eyes looked up at Shylea as she took the creature and set it down on the ground. It raced towards the cage and held hands with one of the other creatures through the bars. Shylea bent down and unlatched the chain.

"Are you insane?" one of the other Cadets whispered. "He'll reprimand us all if you let them go."

"I've followed every order. I'm not following this one. This isn't meant to be another Earth."

"Cadet." Shylea felt the Captain's hot breath on the back of her neck. "Those Christmas trees over there?"

Shylea turned. The Captain barely seemed to notice the cage.

"Christmas trees?" Shylea followed the Captain's gaze. "You mean the tall green things walking around?"

He pulled out a grenade and held it up like it were as innocuous as an ornament. "Yeah. Go chop them down so I can decorate them with baubles. They are in the valley, which is where we should make our settlement anyway."

"They are *walking*, Captain," said Shylea.

He gritted his teeth. "Are you disobeyed an order, Cadet?"

"No, Sir." She took the grenade from his hand.

As she did so, Breanne approached from behind and clobbered the butt of her rifle against the Captain's head. He slumped to the ground among the debris and destruction.

"This is a *new* world," said Breanne.

Shylea kicked the cage open and the creatures scurried out across the charred plains. "And some Earth traditions aren't going to be repeated," she finished off Breanne's sentence.

As if in sync, Breanne turned her weapon on the rest of the soldiers and Shylea rested her finger on the grenade's pin. They looked at each other and smiled.

"Any questions, lads?"

Story behind the stories

The Esky Ghost

This was intended as a reflection of Australian drinking culture. In my day the typical Sunday barbeque lunch was always accompanied by a few drinks, while the kids were off running amuck in the garden. The centrepiece of the adults" barbeque was always the esky (what many Australian's colloquially call "a cooler box" where the beer is kept on ice).
I wanted this story to portray how something typically seen as so harmless can influence the next generation and could result in tragedies such as not watching a child playing by the pool.

Feeding Time

This is a child's interpretation of needing more Time for a terminally ill parent and finding acceptance that when pain is so great that Time is not necessarily a friend to anyone.

Colourblind

Would racism exist if humans didn't perceive colour?

From all that we flee

I wanted to analyse how emotional pain can be so much greater than physical. With an alien race that conveys not only thoughts but telepathically, they can impart all the physical pain to their human captives. However when the tables are turned and the humans have a chance to impart the emotional pain the aliens they don't stand a chance. As a cloned race the pain of losing a child is something they can barely start to comprehend.

Hive mind

This story was initially inspired by watching a stray ant try to pick up the "scent" to find its way back to its "ant line". It's always been an interest in mine how insects that exhibit eusociality know they are part of a "hive mind" or single colony. If such a colony had a higher level of sentience would a separation from this hive mind result in a perception of self and individuality; and how would this newfound awareness shape their purpose and goals.

Look inside

This was a written for an anthology with profits going to charity. The prompt was for "good" terribly written stories. After years of whittling away the convoluted sentences, adverbs and cliché descriptions from my writing this proved surprisingly difficult.

Shadow harvest

If currency was something directly related to survival, such as shadows to shelter people from the sun in a fiery world, would we be so flippant with it.

Tek-tonic

I like the idea that an alien invasion will be something as seemingly innocuous as tiny organisms emerging from a rock that formed during a meteorite crash. Something so small that it isn't even noticed by us.

Attrition of the soul

The concept of downloading one's conscious as data to essentially become immortal has been floating around for a while. I wanted to look at the kind of people who would use it such as those with dementia who wanted to halt the decline and still be able to remember family and how corporations would exploit this potential business.

www.ingramcontent.com/pod-product-compliance
Lightning Source LLC
LaVergne TN
LVHW010615100826
845148LV00014B/2974

* 9 7 8 1 7 6 4 0 1 0 8 5 6 *